ABLE TEAM

AN EXECUTIONER SERIES

Warlord of Azatlan

Dick Stivers

A GOLD EAGLE BOOK FROM

W🌐RLDWIDE

TORONTO • NEW YORK • LONDON • PARIS
AMSTERDAM • STOCKHOLM • HAMBURG
ATHENS • MILAN • TOKYO • SYDNEY

First edition June 1983

ISBN 0-373-61206-0

Copyright © 1983 by Worldwide Library.
Philippine copyright 1983. Australian copyright 1983.

All rights reserved. Except for use in any review, the
reproduction or utilization of this work in whole or in part
in any form by any electronic, mechanical or other means,
now known or hereafter invented, including xerography,
photocopying and recording, or in any information storage
or retrieval system, is forbidden without the permission
of the publisher, Worldwide Library, 225 Duncan Mill Road,
Don Mills, Ontario, Canada M3B 3K9. All the characters in
this book have no existence outside the imagination of the
author and have no relation whatsoever to anyone bearing the
same name or names. They are not even distantly inspired by
any individual known or unknown to the author, and all the
incidents are pure invention.

The Gold Eagle trademark, consisting of the words
GOLD EAGLE and the portrayal of an eagle, and the
Worldwide trademark, consisting of the word
WORLDWIDE in which the letter "O" is represented by a
depiction of a globe, are trademarks of Worldwide Library.

Printed in Canada

The Huey hovered below. He knew it meant death to his friends....

From the clifftop, Gadgets Schwarz looked down on the Huey as it veered in for another attack on the warriors beneath him. Its M-60 flashed fire.

Gadgets dragged a huge roll of barbed wire to the cliff edge. He held it above his head, then threw it.

The roll sailed down in erratic gyrations, unraveling as it fell.

The wire hit the circle of the Huey's rotorblades. It whirled in a tangle above the fuselage, then the blades began to buckle and twist and disintegrate as the wire was sucked into their spin.

The Huey nose-dived into the cliff and exploded.

"I can't believe it!" gasped Gadgets. But his trick had worked. He realized once more that when the military mind eliminated the impossible, whatever remained—however improbable—must be worth a try!

"Dick Stivers makes the reader part of the action. Your blood will race on every page!"
—*New Breed*

Mack Bolan's
ABLE TEAM

Mack Bolan's
PHOENIX FORCE

MACK BOLAN
The Executioner

1

ABOVE THE HORIZON-SPANNING DESERT of Crockett County, Texas, lightning flashed against the sunset. Black thunderheads, touched by red and amber, stood like mountains against the sky.

Sudden raindrops splattered on the windshield of the Dodge. Al Horton, Federal Bureau of Investigation field agent, switched on the wipers. The rain died away as quickly as it had come. Horton flicked off the wiper switch and rolled down the window. The scents of rain and dust and mesquite filled the car.

Two miles ahead on Highway 10, silhouetted against the bloodred western sky, the semi-tractor trailer maintained a steady eighty miles an hour.

Horton glanced at a road map. He eased off on the accelerator. A thin, balding man, forty-three years old with a master's degree in public administration, a father of three children, Horton had no interest in tailgating a truck that was loaded with high-explosive ammunition.

The bureau's San Antonio office had issued a detailed directive to the four agents secretly tailing the truck:

Follow the shipment of weapons and ammunition. If the truck stops, radio the coordinates. If the truck

*stops at an airfield, radio the coordinates, wait for
backup. If the truck nears the Mexican border, radio
the coordinates, wait for backup. Under no circum-
stances attempt to arrest the occupants or seize the
truck's cargo.*

They didn't need to tell us that, Horton thought,
smiling to himself. Four middle-aged office men with
pistols and shotguns against gunrunners with automatic weapons? Right, boss, no heroes this week.

In the rearview mirror, Horton saw the headlights
of the second car. He nudged his partner.

Lou Butterfield awoke, startled. He stared around
blinking at the landscape of sand, creosote bushes
and cactus that blurred past the car. "What's happening? Have they stopped?"

"Not them. What do you say we switch with Allan
and Deihl? Let them take the lead for the next hundred miles?"

Butterfield took the map. He glanced at his watch
then at the odometer to calculate the distance they
had covered while he slept. Then he took the car's
radio microphone. He faked an Old West voice.

"Well, partners, this is Deputy Butterfield. What
say you all mosey on yonder. We'll meet up with ya
at the Pecos."

A voice answered in somber tones. "This is a radio
frequency reserved for the official communications
of federal employees only. Persons engaged in un-
authorized transmissions are subject to prosecution
under sections—"

Laughing, Butterfield cut the other agent off.
"Who is that talkin' back there? Sounds like one of
them dudes from Washington, D.C."

The voice continued. "I will be brief. Will all the would-be cowboys get the hell off?"

"Cuttin' for the trailside," Butterfield continued. "*Hasta la vista*, cowpokes."

Recently transferred from the New York office, Lou Butterfield enjoyed taunting the Texan agents with AM radio cowboy jargon and pranks in the field. As Horton slowed the big Dodge, Butterfield joked about one of his cowboy pranks.

"Remember last month, maybe two months ago, we're following that low-life dope prince around town? And I show up for my shift in the sheriff suit?"

Horton laughed. Butterfield had arrived at the stakeout of the suspect's apartment wearing boots, faded jeans, leather chaps, a plaid shirt, leather vest, lawman's star and a ten-gallon hat. Diehl had threatened Butterfield with on-the-spot dismissal from the bureau if he did not change into a regulation three-piece suit immediately. But Butterfield, knowing from the previous night's monitoring of the phone that the suspect would meet friends at an "Old West" bar, refused to change clothes. At the bar, all the patrons wore phony Western gear. Of the four agents, only Butterfield could enter without inviting stares. He made the arrest, and received a commendation for his foresight in wearing the costume.

The Dodge slowed to a stop on the highway's gravel shoulder. Diehl and Allan sped past in their Volvo station wagon. In the distance, perhaps two or three miles ahead of the semi-tractor trailer they had been following, Horton saw approaching headlights. He thought nothing of it.

Horton walked from the highway, a moist desert wind chilling his sweat-damp slacks and white dress shirt. Around him, he saw the endless expanse of Texas leap from the darkness as lightning flashed.

Emptying his bladder into the sand, he surveyed the panorama of lightning and desert night. He searched the northern sky for the glow of the city lights of Midland and Odessa, more than one hundred miles away. Too early for that, he realized. He looked to the west and saw the last pink streaks of sunset fading from the horizon's storm clouds.

What a great place for a weekend, Horton thought. Rent an RV, take a side road way out to nowhere. Let the boys run wild. Him and Evelyn could carry Julie in a kiddie backpack. Take some long walks. Get away from all this bureau cops-and-robbers crap. Depending on the time of year. Later this month would be great. While it was all green. Before the sun and the heat burned it brown.

On the highway, the headlights of the approaching vehicle passed the semi-truck. The headlights drew nearer the car of the bureau agents following the truck.

Flame flashed from the headlights and the agents' Volvo exploded. The churning ball of gasoline fire rolled across the desert as the gutted car careered out of control.

"Butterfield!" Horton screamed. "The radio! They killed Allan and Diehl—"

Horton's smooth-soled wingtipped shoes slipped in the sand. He stumbled to his hands and knees, felt cactus spines jab his leg. At last he sprinted back to the Dodge.

Staring at the column of smoke in the distance, his eyes wide with panic, Butterfield was shouting into the microphone.

"This is Agent Butterfield on Highway Ten. They just rocketed the lead car. Repeat, rocketed. Diehl and Allan are dead. And now they're coming for us...."

"Out!" Horton screamed at his partner. "Get your shotgun."

Horton grabbed his eight-shot Ithaca 12-gauge from under a blanket on the back seat. He paused only to take a flashlight, then ran for the open desert.

Behind him, Butterfield shouted the number of highway miles from the last town, Ozona. Then he, too, grabbed his shotgun and sprinted through the gravel and mesquite.

"They said at least fifteen minutes before they can get a helicopter out here."

"Out there," Horton corrected him, pointing into the desert.

"Right!"

They ran through the darkness, distant lightning flashes throwing long shadows behind them. Horton, more agile and more familiar with Texas terrain, led the way. He dashed through gaps in the creosote brush, following the white pathways of sand. A lightning flash revealed the black slash of a gully.

Horton stepped off into it, sidesliding a few feet to the tangle of dry weeds and sand at the bottom. Butterfield hopped down an instant later.

A rocket shrieked. Punching through the Dodge, the warhead sprayed thousands of bits of exploding white-hot fragments into the night. An instant later, flames engulfed the hulk.

Tires screeched as a four-wheel-drive pickup fish-tailed to a stop on the asphalt. Four autoweapons flashed from the back of the pickup, the gunmen sweeping the burning Dodge and the roadside with bursts.

Crouching low in the gully, the two FBI agents ran north. Overweight and out of shape, Butterfield panted, stumbled. Acrid black soot from their burning car's tires clouded into the air above them. They heard the *clang-crump* of 40mm grenades.

Horton caught his partner's shoulder and shoved him against the gully side. He put a hand into the sand and silt to find moisture.

"Rub this mud on my shirt," Horton whispered. He slapped the white short-sleeved dress shirt he wore.

Butterfield understood. He wore a dark sports coat over his white shirt. But Horton, in bleached and starched white, would stand out like a beacon.

They slapped mud on one another, on their faces and shirts, as the pickup bounced over the desert. His face masked desert-brown, Horton eased his eyes above the gully.

Against the light of the flaming car, he saw a skirmish line of four men heading toward them. The truck paced them, high beams and side-mounted spotlights bathing the desert. A weapon popped from the pickup bed.

No, not a weapon, not a rocket or a grenade launcher, Horton realized as a white sun seared away the night.

A flare.

He turned to Butterfield and saw him staring up at

the blazing magnesium. "Don't look at it! It'll kill your night-vision—"

"Oh, God, Al," Butterfield groaned. "We're up against paramilitaries...."

"It's all right, it's all right. It's a big desert and they only have fifteen minutes to find us. We don't have to shoot it out. We just have to stay out of sight."

Slugs ripped through the brush above them. Butterfield flinched, then scrambled away on his hands and knees, dragging his shotgun through the sand and grit. The barrel and stock clattered on rocks. The shadows around him shifted rhythmically as the flare swung on the end of its miniature parachute.

Horton waited until the flare sputtered out, then ran after Butterfield. He heard another flare pop. He threw himself down on his panicked friend. As the second flare's white glare lit the area, Horton held Butterfield down and whispered to him.

"Don't move while the flares are up. They can only see us if we move while the flares are up. It's a big desert, thousands of square miles, they can't find us. Keep cool, they can't find us."

Autobursts ripped through the brush. High-velocity slugs zipped into the distance. Ricochets hummed past. They heard the *clang-pop* of more 40mm grenades. A grenade rushed over them, exploded twenty yards away. Bits of steel showered them.

"They're just shooting wild, it's just dumb shit recon-by-fire. Wait until the flare...."

Darkness returned. Horton ran again, keeping his back below the level of the gully walls. He heard Butterfield stumbling behind him.

Shotgun blast! Horton threw himself flat as another flare burst above him. He looked back to see Butterfield crawling over a tangle of rocks and windblown creosote branches.

He knew what had happened. Butterfield had fallen and hit his shotgun on a rock. Ithacas do not have a dependable safety. Cocked and with a round in the chamber, the weapon had discharged.

Horton pumped his weapon to chamber the first shotshell. Now they would fight. Because of Butterfield's stumbling and the accidental discharge, they would fight. Two men with .38 pistols and shotguns against a squad of paramilitary gunmen with automatic weapons and grenades and illumination. Horton thought of abandoning Butterfield to die alone. No. Never.

Never leave your wounded, never leave your men to the enemy. Horton could not disobey his Airborne discipline, no matter how many years ago the Fort Ord instructors had screamed the words into his head. He could not leave a man he had worked with for months, who had covered him, who had faced death in the doorways and alleys of the drug world with him. Bursts of high-velocity slugs ripped over them. Twigs fell, rocks clattered. A grenade popped only a few feet away, the shrapnel tearing through the brush above them. But the gully sheltered them.

Horton attempted a joke. "Get with it, partner. This is the shoot-out. Make them eat lead."

As the flarelight sputtered away, Horton crawled to the gully side. He looked up. He saw the flashing barrel of a gunman silhouetted against the 4WD's headlights. Pushing in his Ithaca's safety, he put the shotgun's front sight on the center of the gunman's chest, and squeezed the trigger.

The man dropped. Horton slid down as burst after burst searched for him. A grenade flashed, throwing dirt and chopped mesquite over him. Butterfield crawled to him. Horton gave him commands in a hiss.

"Keep moving! That way. Dump the sand out of that barrel before you try to fire it."

Butterfield tried to speak, but could not. Horton shoved him on as bullets puffed dust only an arm's length above them.

A form jumped into the gully. Horton lay still, watching the darkness, his shotgun on line.

Light bathed the brush and rocks. Horton saw a shoulder and the side of a head above a tangle, twenty yards away. He sighted, and he waited.

The gunman raised his M-16. Horton fired a blast of Number Six birdshot into the man's face.

Screaming, his face and part of a hand gone, the gunman thrashed in the dust. Blood sprayed from his destroyed mouth as he called out in Spanish to the others.

Horton pumped his weapon to chamber another round, and waited for the flarelight to give him another target.

The air above him exploded with shrapnel and slugs. A heavy-caliber machine gun hammered at the gully, the dirt exploding with the impacts of slugs and grenade blasts.

Behind Horton, Butterfield fired his shotgun once, twice. Then a tight-throated whine became a scream as an autoburst raked Butterfield's legs. Horton scrambled as he saw a form with a flashing muzzle.

Raising his shotgun, Horton fired at the same instant as his target, hundreds of tiny lead balls racing to kill the gunman even as a 40mm fragmentation grenade struck only inches from Horton's feet.

His legs were instantly shredded. Blood gushed from a thousand wounds. He struggled to work the shotgun's pump action. But his left arm did not function.

Dropping the shotgun, he jerked the .38 pistol from the holster at the small of his back.

A boot stomped down on his arm. Horton looked up into the muzzle of an M-16. He never saw the flash, never felt the burst that ended his life.

2

Gray in the first minutes of dawn, the boulevards, parks and public buildings of Washington, D.C. wheeled below as the Air Force jet banked and took a route to the south-southwest.

Hermann "Gadgets" Schwarz, electronics and communications specialist for Able Team, looked to the east. He saw the incandescent disk of the sun rising above light-marked suburbs in Maryland and Delaware. Headlights streaked the expressways as commuters traveled to the capital. The ex-Green Beret radioman, veteran of wars in Southeast Asia, the Americas and the Middle East, smiled at the irony.

All we government employees, on our way to work. You to your offices. Me to—

"Guatemala," Andrzej Konzaki said from the conference table. The wide-shouldered, legless ex-Marine put a pointer to Central America. "You'll be landing in five hours at Guatemala International."

"This an official visit?" Rosario Blancanales asked. A calm, quiet ex-Green Beret born in Puerto Rico, Blancanales served as medic, interpreter and indigenous operations specialist for Able Team. Like Gadgets, Blancanales still wore his pajamas. The call to Stony Man had awakened them at 4:00 A.M.

Carl Lyons interrupted before Konzaki could answer Blancanales. The cynical ex-LAPD officer, hardened and scarred by wars in the streets of Los Angeles, and more recently in the secret dirty wars fought by Able Team, had a reputation that did not include courtesy.

"What does Guatemala have to do with Texas? The call said something happened in Texas."

"To paraphrase an old English preacher," Konzaki told them. " 'No nation is an island.' Even those surrounded by water. Not anymore. What happened is this. . . ."

Konzaki read from a notebook of photocopied documents and top-secret memos. "Throughout the past several months, in fact the last few years, the FBI has been working on several gangs running weapons into Central America. They've traced the serial numbers of weapons captured in El Salvador back to Miami and Los Angeles—"

"Commies are killing people with American weapons?" Lyons broke in.

"Everybody's killing people with American weapons," Konzaki told him. "Castro took Cuba with M-1s, Thompsons and Brownings. The Sandinistas took Nicaragua with rifles bought in Miami gunshops."

"First good reason I've ever heard for gun control." Lyons took off a pale blue sports coat, then unbuttoned his bright red shirt. His pager had beeped from the bedside of a young woman in Georgetown; he had taken a taxi to the airport to wait for the others to arrive by helicopter from the Great Smoky Mountains.

Konzaki continued. "The FBI have a special task force of officers following the flow of weapons from the United States to the death squads in El Salvador. We're trying to stop those crazies before they murder everyone down there.

"What the FBI have found are huge shipments of ammunition and weapons going south. Not just pistols and rifles. Machine guns, grenades, rockets. Tons of ammunition—"

"Sounds like someone's going into politics," Lyons joked.

The interruptions irritated Konzaki. He stared at Lyons for a moment, then looked to the others. "How do we shut him up? I've got a briefing to deliver, and you've only got five hours before you hit the ground."

Blancanales considered the question. "Shoot him. Back when one of those bikers on Catalina got lucky and hit him with a slug from an M-60, I didn't see Lyons moving or talking for at least two minutes. It was all he could do to breathe—"

Gadgets disagreed. "Don't shoot him. He's a good pointman. Always blundering into things, stirring up trouble long before we show up. Gives us time to plan something intelligent. Maybe we could kick him in the head for a while—"

"Tell you what, Konzaki," Lyons ended the jiving. "You don't like me talking, kick my ass."

Blancanales and Gadgets went silent, waiting for the ex-Marine's response.

Konzaki had lost both legs during the Tet Offensive. He stared at Lyons. The others waited for rage or mayhem. But Konzaki merely laughed.

"Why should I break up my good plastic feet on your worthless body? However, I just might twist your head off if you don't shut your mouth. Now will you let me proceed?"

Lyons laughed too. He said nothing as Konzaki flipped through pages. Mack Bolan's primo weapon-smith continued to summarize the documents and reports for Able Team. "Yesterday a semi-tractor trailer left a Houston warehouse. The task force had agents in cars following the truck, plus men and helicopters waiting as backup. Out in the desert, the cars got hit. The last radio transmission from the agents reported rockets. Apparently the lead car got hit, then the gunmen got the second car. When the backup teams got to the scene, they found both cars burning. The first two agents never knew what hit them. The other two men died in the desert. Somehow they got away from their car before they got rocketed.

"The agents fought with shotguns and .38 pistols. The gang hit them with military weapons. The backup officers found 5.56mm brass, 7.62 NATO, M-60 belt links, 40mm grenade casings.

"The agents must have wounded or killed a few of them. There were several blood trails. But after both officers were wounded, the gang overran them and executed them with point-blank riflefire. Then they mutilated them, and left them for the backup officers to find."

"And we're following the gang?" Lyons asked, his voice quiet.

Konzaki nodded. Blancanales asked the next question: "How do we know they're in Guatemala?"

"National Security Agency satellites tracked a flight, probably a turbo-prop cargo plane, from Texas to Guatemala. It landed in the State of Q-U-I-C-H-E, pronounced key- chay, in the interior of Guatemala.

"Clouds blocked the satellites from photographing the exact landing area, but chances are the gang has an airstrip and warehouses up there somewhere.

"The killings in Texas ruined what looked like a successful conclusion to an investigation spanning years. But you men will have the benefit of all the information acquired.

"We may not know the names of the men who pulled the triggers and did the cutting, but we know who hired them. His name is Klaust de la Unomundo-Stiglitz, a Guatemalan billionaire known in that country by his Spanish name, Unomundo. Here are photos of him."

Konzaki passed out photos and folders of biographical details. "He's blond because his father was German, a Nazi SS officer on the run after the victory in Europe. He married a debutante from one of the wealthiest families in the country.

"It wasn't enough for Unomundo to be born rich. After college in Germany, he went straight into his father's business. He multiplied his inheritance through drug and weapons smuggling.

"This punk was not subtle. The FBI knew about him from the start. But he ran a tight organization, a Spanish-speaking Mafia with a Gestapo philosophy.

"No one crossed him and lived. One time, one of his managers went to Miami with a set of account books. He said he'd cooperate with the U.S. Justice Department to break a transnational scam if they'd help him get his family out of Guatemala. But our people couldn't locate his wife or kids.

"One day, the accountant gets a big set of photos. They showed his wife and kids hanging by their arms, going down slow, an inch at a time, one photo at a time, into tubs of acid. The guy killed himself the same day.

"Unomundo took over his father's companies. He made billions, invested billions in land in Guatemala, El Salvador and Mexico, in manufacturing and transportation industries throughout Central America. He used his winning ways—extortion, murder, terror—to build up his financial empire. His death squads wiped out unions, competitors and government officials.

"He also invested in politicians. His death squads worked for his politicians to make sure they took power. Sometimes the killers passed themselves off as right wing, sometimes as Communists. But it was always murder-for-money.

"We have reports of his influence—meaning money and weapons—spreading to very powerful right-wing leaders. That's where we thought his weapons went to. But then we got information on other shipments, other weapons.

"Here's a satellite photo of a ship off the Guatemalan coast. That's a Huey. Here's another. A Cobra gunship in flight to the central mountains of Guatemala. These helicopters are a mystery.

"If we spotted them going into Guatemala two years ago, we could have understood. The Carter Administration cut off Guatemala'a purchases of American weapons because of the old government's human rights violations. No helicopters, no rifles, no ammunition, nothing.

"So the government went to other countries for their weapons. The Guatemalans are damned proud people and they don't take flack from anyone. They don't allow other countries to dictate their politics.

"But now there's a new government. The younger army officers rebelled against the generals and threw out the general who was in office. They gave the presidency to the man who actually won the elections in 1974.

"In 1974, after he'd won the popular vote, the generals invalidated his election and drove him into exile. Eventually he came back, but stayed out of politics. He worked for his church and became a pastor. Story is that he was sweeping out the church when the young officers came to ask him to be president of Guatemala. Then things changed. Overnight, no more death squads. No more disappearances. No more torture.

"Now the U.S. Congress is planning new aid programs. Our President has already sent the Guatemalan president the spare parts the army needed for its helicopters, and it's only a matter of months before the Guatemalans get everything they need. But in fact the Guatemalans aren't asking for anything. They've got a war going on in the mountains with the Cuban, Nicaraguan and Marxist crazies, but the Guatemalans will fight it with rocks before they beg anyone for help.

"That's why we don't understand about the Hueys and Cobras. The Guatemalan army doesn't need to buy them on the international market. Maybe next week they could get the helicopters at a Congressional discount. We thought maybe they were going to the Salvadoran army, as an indirect way of getting around the liberals in Washington. But they haven't shown up there."

Lyons pointed to the satellite photos. "How do you know it's this Unomundo who's smuggling the helicopters?"

"You figure it out. He's running tons of 7.62 NATO prepacked in canisters for gunship mini-Gatlings. Either the helicopters are his, or he's supplying whoever's got them. What you men have to do is go in and close him down. The Guatemalans are allowing you into the country because his gang hit FBI men."

"Then we're official?" Blancanales asked.

"Semi-official. You'll have a liaison officer, cars, and people working behind the scenes to keep the army and police away from Quiche long enough for you to find his airstrip and stockpiles. Hit the gang, destroy the weapons, hit Unomundo.

"But remember—the Guatemalans are going way out on the international limb to let you chase Unomundo, hot pursuit or not. If the newpapers or the international media find out about you three, it could be a real embarrassment to the new Guatemalan government. So if you can't do this quick and clean and very, very discreetly, you pull out. The Guatemalans will take the job over. Agreed?"

The three men of Able Team nodded.

"Lyons, you understand?" Konzaki stressed. "We've gotten some reports of very extreme behavior in Cairo. We sent you there to resolve a problem and you liquidated the problem.''

"Resolve, liquidate, what's the difference?''

"Torture is not the American way.''

"You weren't there!'' Lyons snapped back. "I explained it all to Mack. Even he went with it. It had to happen.''

"Mack said that?'' Konzaki asked.

"It wasn't torture. Justice and torture are two different things. And victory is something else entirely. You'll never see me pulling some crap just to make someone hurt. But you'll never see me stop when someone's between me and the mission. You understand that?''

"All right, all right,'' Konzaki nodded. Enough had been said. "Here are maps. Satellite photos of the topography of Quiche. A dictionary of the language. The mass of the people don't speak Spanish. Maybe the village leaders and the merchants speak Spanish.''

"Key-chay, key-chay, key-chay,'' Lyons repeated, learning to say the unfamiliar word.

"Here's a book on the life-styles of the Indians, here's a book on their traditional weaving, here's a book on modern Guatemala.''

Blancanales took the weaving book and leafed through the color illustrations of Indian men and women in Mayan clothes. Painted in watercolors, the illustrations captured scenes from a culture that predated the civilizations of Europe. Women wore designs thousands of years old, men sported the same costumes their ancestors wore to battle the Spanish marauders. They had lost their freedom not because of ignorance or poverty or weakness, but because they did not have the modern weapons of the Europeans. The Mayans had only copper and gold knives against steel swords and armor, only stone clubs and arrows against muskets and cannons. Hence they became slaves.

Yet the Mayan culture survived the long horror of the European overlords. With the Revolution, all Guatemalans—those descended from the Spanish masters and those who had survived as property—became citizens of a New World nation, equal under the law, yet as different and distinct as peoples from different planets.

As he leafed through the pages, Blancanales heard someone's breath catch. Lyons was staring over his partner's shoulder, his eyes fixed on the paintings of lovely mahogany-skinned women, proud barrel-chested men, children playing in priceless handwoven clothes that in North America would only be seen in museums.

Even Gadgets, the technological wizard, stared. "The places we go, wowie-zowie."

"Here are your weapons," Konzaki announced, lifting a large fiberboard carrying case onto the conference table.

Blancanales gave the book to Lyons and turned his attention to the gear they would carry into the mountains of Guatemala.

Konzaki passed him an M-16/M-203 hybrid assault-rifle and grenade launcher. The rifle part of the over-and-under weapon fired 5.56mm slugs in single shots, three-round bursts, or full-auto through the new quick-twist NATO barrel. The lower tube fired 40mm grenades. In addition to the three-mode sear mechanism, the Stony Man weaponsmith had added luminous nightsights.

"With buckshot rounds?" Blancanales asked.

Konzaki nodded. He took out a Heckler & Koch MP-5SD3 submachine gun. A small weapon that fired 9mm slugs, the weapon featured integral silencing and Starlite scope. "Notice the scope mounts. They're quick-release, positive-lock. If the going gets rough, put the Starlite in its protective case. And here's the Atchisson."

The weaponsmith lifted out Lyons's favorite assault weapon. Looking much like a standard M-16, but heavier, larger, the Atchisson fired twelve-gauge shells in semi-auto, three-shot burst, or full-auto modes from a seven-round box magazine. Konzaki hand-loaded the shells, cramming a mixed load of double-ought and Number Two steel balls into each shell.

"Hey, Ironman," Gadgets jived. "Your true love just made her entrance—"

Lyons didn't take his eyes from the colors and Mayan faces of the book.

"Hey! Listen up!" Konzaki ordered.

"What?"

"Briefing isn't over yet. Here's your LCKD—The Lyons Crowd Killing Device," he said as he passed the Atchisson across the aisle. "Pay attention, or someday you just might not come back."

"Someday I might find someplace I don't want to come back from."

"Look at him," Gadgets told the others. "He likes that book."

"I like what I see. Maybe this is the place I don't come back from."

"Ironman the Romantic," Gadgets laughed.

"And Mr. Schwarz," Konzaki continued. "You're carrying the radios and electronic gear. We thought of assembling the same package of components you took into the Amazon, but I rejected the idea. Anywhere in Guatemala, you've only a three- or four-hour drive from phones with microwave links to international lines."

"Thank God. That satellite radio must've weighed fifty pounds on its own."

"Everything else is standard. The Beretta 93-Rs. Radio detonators and a kilo of C-4. Battle armor. Bandoliers. Ten thousand dollars cash for expenses. Except for the long guns, everything's in backpacks, ready for a hike. So, gentlemen, questions?"

Lyons looked from the beauty of the Mayans to the weapons, the ammunition, the explosives. He looked at the other military gear. An uncharacteristic sadness touched his face. Then his eyes returned to the book. He read the strange and beautiful words aloud:

"Qui-che. So-lo-la. Cak-chi-quel. Tzu-tu-jil."

"And Lyons, remember what Bolan told you," Konzaki concluded. "Put your *mind* into your work. No recklessness."

3

Smoke swirled from burning cornfields and obscured the valleys. In the ninety seconds of their approach to La Aurora International Airport, Able Team saw volcanoes crowned with clouds, jungle patterned by scorched fields and yellow-dust roads, the raw earth of new subdivisions carved from the hills and ravines around Guatemala City. Then their jet's wheels screeched on the blacktop.

The jet taxied past the passenger terminal and continued down the runway to the private and corporate planes at the far end of the field. Passing parked Pipers, Beechcrafts and Lear jets, the pilot halted their plane only a few steps from an open hangar.

Konzaki said farewell to the three men of Able Team. "See you next week. Do the best you can and be discreet."

"We'll get him." Lyons shook Konzaki's hand, then dodged a friendly punch. He lifted his backpack and the fiberboard case concealing his Atchisson, and went to the cabin door.

"One last question," Blancanales asked Konzaki. "If the Guatemalans are so nationalistic and proud, why are they allowing us into the country?"

"Like I told you, hot pursuit. Also—" Konzaki glanced out the ports, saw field workers pushing stairs to the jet's door "—they think Unomundo's people might have infiltrated their security organizations. If they mounted an action, his spies would know. But if three North Americans drop out of the sky...."

Gadgets looked to Blancanales. "My paranoia meter just red-lined. If Unomundo has spies in the police and army, why not in our liaison group. Like in Cairo...."

Months before, agents of the fanatical Muslim Brotherhood had penetrated a secret U.S. Air Force operation in Cairo. With precise information on personnel and activities, the Muslims had plotted attacks and finally killed several Americans. Stony Man dispatched Able Team to Egypt, not to investigate the murders but to shadow the joint CIA/Egyptian task force investigating the acts of terrorism. In one long day and night of unrelenting action, Able Team smashed the Muslim fanatics. In a flaming climax, they tricked the Egyptian liaison who was betraying the Americans into betraying himself.

"Ironman, what do you think?" Gadgets asked Lyons.

"I think I don't like it. Andy, can we ditch our liaison?"

"That's up to you. You three are the men working the operation. You make the decisions."

The cabin door opened. Midday tropical glare and the roar of jet engines cut off the discussion. Lyons saw two Chevy Silverado vans—one-ton pickups built for nine passengers—parked inside a hangar. Two men in sport suits waited there.

Pausing on the aluminum steps to put on his sun

glasses, Lyons scanned the immediate area. Directly in front of him, only twenty steps away, their Guatemalan liaison officers waited. Lyons looked to the hangars on the right and left.

He saw no technicians at the parked planes, no airport workers moving in the other hangars. A truck had its hood open. A tarp on one fender protected the paint from tools and parts, but he saw no mechanic. In another area, a pickup truck idled, cargo stacked in the back, smoke wisping from the exhaust pipe, the driver's door hanging open. A step from the truck, fizzing pink pop spread from a bottle, sunlight glinting from the bottle as it rolled on the concrete.

Lyons put his right hand behind his back, snapped his fingers to get his partners' attention, then straightened his forefinger and made the motion of cocking his thumb back like a pistol hammer.

"Receiving on your wavelength," Gadgets answered. "No video transmission necessary. We got the picture."

As Lyons clanged down the steps, his partners stayed in the jet. Blancanales turned to Gadgets. "When I walk down there, I'm going to embrace our brother officers of the law. Have any small gifts I can give them? So that I can always hear their voices?"

"Electronic *abrazos*?" Gadgets asked. Blancanales nodded.

As Lyons stepped into the hangar's shade, the senior officer, a dignified middle-aged Hispanic wearing an expensive European-styled suit, white peppering his short black hair, extended a strong hand.

"Colonel Morales," the officer told him. He motioned the second man forward. Younger, his shoulders thrown back in military stature, the other man also wore a tailored suit. A gold wristwatch flashed at his cuff.

"Captain Merida."

"Pleasure to meet you," Lyons assured them. "Let's hope we do this business quickly. I know you don't appreciate our troubles coming to your country."

"Yes, we will be quick," Captain Merida told him.

Lyons looked back. He saw Gadgets and Blancanales finally leave the jet. "My partners."

"Only three men?" Colonel Morales asked. He waved toward the two nine-seat trucks. "We were told to expect a team. We thought—"

Blancanales greeted the officers in Spanish, throwing his arms around them as if meeting lifelong friends. The officers politely returned the masculine embraces, then introduced themselves. They turned to Gadgets and shook hands, and introduced themselves in English to him. Finally, Captain Merida motioned toward one of the Silverado war wagons.

"We have far to go. It is already the afternoon."

"Where we going?" Lyons asked.

"To Unomundo," Merida answered.

"You know where he is?"

"We will search."

Lyons looked to the others. "Pol, Wizard. The man may operate up in the hills, but he's got to have people in the city here. Transport, communication, spies in the government, whatever. Perhaps Colonel Morales and Captain Merida might have leads on Unomundo units here. I say we don't go into the mountains cold."

"Is it possible we could gain information from the criminals here?" Blancanales asked the officers. "Before going into the mountains?"

The colonel smiled. "*Claro*. Of course. In truth, there is one man who we intended to arrest today. A bus driver. He carries messages. We will go to the bus station."

"What about others?" Lyons pressed.

"If not that one, we will take some other. There are many."

Able Team stowed their gear in one of the trucks and got in, Lyons in the front, Gadgets and Blancanales lounging in the middle seat. Captain Merida started the Silverado. They drove into the afternoon glare.

Gadgets glanced back and saw the colonel go to an office. Then they cut between the hangars and continued to an access lane. Gadgets looked over to Blancanales. His partner tapped the tiny plastic phone that was plugged into his ear, and he smiled. In the front seat, Lyons tried to make conversation with Captain Merida.

"This Unomundo character caught our security forces by surprise. How does he operate down here?"

"He is unknown," Merida answered. He followed the narrow lane to a perimeter road. They passed parked cars and pickups. In the several colors of airline companies, technicians moved in equipment yards, or drove service trucks. Administrators in white shirts and ties talked with workers.

"Our officer told us Unomundo has links to the other Central American countries," Lyons continued. "What do you know about the foreigners?"

"Yes, many foreigners."

They came to a guard booth. A man in a suit waved them through the gate. Lyons turned in the front seat and looked back. He saw the man leave the guard booth. A potbellied policeman stepped from a doorway. He wore a uniform of baggy blue pants and a frayed light blue shirt, and carried an M-1 carbine. The man in the suit ignored the policeman, went instead to a new Dodge sedan.

Lyons saw Gadgets make the same observation. Gadgets met Lyons's eyes, touched his ear, looked over to Blancanales. Lyons did not understand.

"Later," Gadgets explained.

Following a street to a major boulevard, Captain Merida turned east. Immaculate parkways bright with tropical flowers separated the east-west lanes. New American and European cars competed with trucks and rattling buses for the two lanes flowing east, the cars swerving in and out of traffic with seemingly divine protection. Fumes grayed the air. At every other corner, diesel smoke clouded behind buses pulling away from bus stops.

They came to a traffic circle, from which they traveled north.

Shops, auto dealers, office buildings linked both sides of the avenue. People crowded the sidewalks. Knots of shoppers and workers waited for buses on the corners. Pedestrians dashed through stop-and-go traffic to the grassy islands that divided the north-south lanes.

The North Americans of Able Team saw Guatemalans of all social classes and ethnic origins

Mayan, European, and mixed heritage Ladinos. They saw garage workers in grease-caked coveralls. Office workers in slacks and shirts. Businessmen in Mercedes sedans. Vendors pushing handcarts painted with garish ice cream cones.

Two young businessmen talked at a curb as they attempted to wave down a taxi. Both wore the gray-suit, dark-tie uniform of junior executives. Both held the required briefcases. One had fair hair and European features, the other black hair and a profile seen on the walls of Mayan temples.

Indians walked in the modern crowds. At a traffic light, Lyons studied a Mayan woman. Shoulder to shoulder between a teenage girl in a disco-red jump suit and a technician with the logo of a multinational corporation on his uniform, the Indian woman waited for a bus. She wore sandals on her calloused, dusty feet, a simple wrap-shirt of broadloomed fabric, a *huipile*—he knew the word from the books—of hand-woven yellow and blues and purples, designs brocaded into the fabric, then highlighted with embroidered details. The cloth and designs and colors were a tapestry of ancient culture: history, tradition, and artistry displayed simultaneously in the marvelous fabric. Even with his ignorance of weaving and needlework, Lyons knew the woman wore months of work.

She saw him staring. Her proud, austere face returned his gaze. She saw only another North American in an automobile, his face like all the others, his sports coat and shirt like the clothes all the others wore, the automobile only one of millions from a factory. She found him uninteresting, and looked away.

Lyons saw her disdain and disinterest, and he laughed at himself. Captain Merida glanced over to him and misinterpreted his laughter. The light changed and he accelerated through the intersection as he commented: "Soon, all those filthy Indians will be gone."

Lyons said nothing.

Continuing north on the modern Avenida la Reforma, Captain Merida followed the flow of traffic without speeding or swerving to exploit open lanes. Able Team watched the city pass, turning in their seats to sightsee like tourists.

Gadgets spotted a familiar Dodge sedan. He had seen it before, parked at the airport's guard booth. The man who had waved them through the security gate was driving the sedan. With a glance, Gadgets indicated the car to Blancanales. Blancanales nodded, touched his earphone.

The Reforma passed under a railroad bridge, then they saw a modern civic center of plazas and public buildings. Sidewalk vendors displayed fruits and nuts. Families herded coveys of children. Roller skaters weaved through the crowds. Soldiers with rifles guarded the offices of the Banco de Guatemala. A street preacher held up a Bible and delivered a sermon to a group of onlookers.

Above them, on a hill overlooking the plazas and government offices, they saw a fantasy of free-form concrete: the *Teatro Nacional*.

A boulevard intersected the Reforma at a diagonal. Captain Merida eased left through the honking, screeching traffic. He then turned left again. Now they drove south. Lyons saw the west side of the *Teatro Nacional*. He looked into the shadows to double-check, finally asked the captain,

"Where are we going?"

"*El terminal de autobuses* . . . the bus station."

"But we've gone in a circle."

"The traffic is bad. I go around to save time. Do not worry, we will be there very soon."

They drove through an older section of the city. Diesel-blackened buildings housed workshops, small stores, second- and third-floor apartments. Trucks jammed narrow side streets. Buses that were crowded solid with passengers, goods and produce lashed to the roof racks, low-geared up slight inclines. Captain Merida turned left again to follow a sidestreet for three blocks.

Parked buses lined the streets. Vendors sold vegetables and fruit and manufactured trinkets on blankets spread in the gutters. Five-foot-tall laborers staggered under hundred-pound bags of grain, only their back and a headstrap carrying the loads. Soldiers in combat gear double-parked a jeep and began to unload cases of empty pop bottles at the warehouse of a soft-drink wholesaler. Captain Merida waited patiently for the soldiers to finish and drive away, then continued on.

Buses and trucks blocked a street. A policeman directed Merida to turn. Going right, he saw a gap in the parked cars, and he swerved over to park.

A street vendor's cart occupied the space. The toothless old man put up a hand to halt the truck; he motioned Merida away. Merida took out his wallet and opened it to show a badge and an identification card. But the old man had already turned his back on them.

"Perro anciano!" Captain Merida called out. But in the noise and chaos of the trucks and buses and crowded sidewalks, the old man could not, or would not, hear him.

Throwing the truck into neutral and jerking the parking brake, Captain Merida stepped out. They saw him wave his identification in the old man's face. When the old man talked back, Merida slapped him down, then kicked him. People crowded around as the young man in the expensive suit dragged the old man off the asphalt and threw him against the hand cart. A young laborer stepped forward to defend the old peddler. The captain's identification stopped him. The laborer helped the old man push his cart away.

Meanwhile, Blancanales had leaned forward to Lyons. Motioning Gadgets to listen also, Blancanales whispered:

"At the hangar, I put a microtransmitter in Colonel Morales's front coat pocket. He's spent the last half hour on the phone arranging for us to be kidnapped and murdered. It'll happen here."

Captain Merida returned to park the truck. He smiled to the North Americans. "Come, my friends. We will go learn of Unomundo."

4

A THOUSAND ODORS STRUCK THEM. The perfumes of flowers and citrus. The stink of caged chickens and tethered pigs. The rot of vegetables and fruits mashed under thousands of sandals. Diesel soot from the buses. All mixed and fermented under a sun that blazed on a land only fifteen degrees north of the Equator.

Watching for the men who would kill them, Lyons and Blancanales followed Captain Merida through the market stalls. The narrow passages were claustrophobic with crowding Indians and Ladinos, with overhanging awnings and piled goods.

Lyons and Blancanales scanned the faces and hands of the people, watching for weapons or sudden movement. The confusion of colors and faces and objects threatened to overwhelm their danger-heightened perception.

Voices called out to them in Spanish. Women talked to one another in guttural Indian languages. Children whistled and pointed at the North Americans, chattering to them in languages Lyons had never heard before. Animals squealed. Cassette players and radios blared a cacophony of music and songs.

Gadgets had stayed in the Silverado, supposedly to

watch their weapons and gear. Actually he had hot-
wired the vehicle and now waited for a signal to move.
Lyons wore his earphone, and kept his hand-radio
channel open for instant communication. Blancanales
still monitored the microtransmitter in Colonel
Morales's pocket.

The *Terminal de Autobuses Extraurbanos* occupied
a block-square section of the city. The crowded markets surrounded the terminal itself, an asphalt area
where the buses shuttling from the villages to the capital exchanged passengers and loads. Leaving the market stalls behind, the three men came to the buses.

The designers of the terminal complex had built it
in accordance with Third World realities. There were
no ticket offices, no waiting rooms, no service
garages. The drivers collected the fares, passengers
waited on the buses, mechanics worked on engines
and brakes and transmissions while the waiting passengers supervised. Pay lavatories offered privacy to
those with five centavos. The poor used the corners
and the gutters.

The air was gray with diesel exhaust. Hundreds of
Ford and Chevrolet and Bluebird buses jammed the
blacktop. Rows of buses, parked side by side, only
inches separating one bus from the next, waited for
passengers. Passengers carrying burdens of packages
and sacks and children wandered along the rows
searching for the buses that would take them to their
villages. Drivers waited behind the wheels or tinkered
with engines as assistants lashed goats and furniture
and bundles to roof racks. Other assistants, shouting
over the noise of radios and horns and blaring rock
and roll, announced the names of cities and villages.

"Xela!"

"Chi-Chi!"

"Antigua!"

"Sacatepequez!"

"Nebaj!"

Arriving and departing buses eased through the chaos of the narrow lanes, assistants walking a step ahead of the front bumpers to part the chaos of crowding people and other maneuvering buses. Assistants guided drivers into narrow spaces with slaps on the fender: two slaps to continue, three quick slaps to stop.

A few steps behind Merida and Lyons, Blancanales lifted his coat as if to glance into an interior pocket, and whispered into his concealed hand-radio.

"Political to Ironman and the Wizard. I'm getting traffic sounds from the colonel. Must be on his way with his hit team. Wizard, we're in the terminal. Zero this far. No shadows, no badguys. Zero."

"Nothing here," Gadgets answered. "But I'm cocked and unlocked."

His partners' voices whispered in his earphone as Lyons followed Merida. The officer glanced back to the North Americans from time to time as he led them through the crowds. He read the hand-lettered destination signs of buses.

A teenaged assistant called out to Lyons in awkward English: "Okay, man. Where you want to go? We go. Cheap. Anywhere you—"

The teenager saw Merida. His voice stopped in mid-sentence. Looking from the Guatemalan officer to the North American, the teenager stepped back between two buses and disappeared.

Lyons saw other bus drivers and assistants spot Merida. Most of the men and teenagers carefully ignored the officer. Others went quiet as the Guatemalan in the expensive suit passed. Lyons, with his years as a uniformed police officer, then as a plainclothes detective, knew the reactions: the people recognized Merida as a police officer, and they hated him.

But why would they hate Merida? Unlike the pimps and dealers and male prostitutes who had despised Lyons because he represented law and decency, these bus drivers and their teenage assistants worked for a living, they sweated long hours behind the steering wheels of their buses or under the hoods repairing the engines. In the United States, bus and truck drivers joined police officers at the same all-night hamburger stands and doughnuts shops, sharing stories and jokes, often exchanging information. Why would it be different here?

A driver saw Lyons, smiled and motioned him over. Another man hissed to the driver, nodding toward Merida. The driver's face went hard, his eyes narrowing as he linked Lyons and Blancanales to Captain Merida. Lyons took a step toward the driver, only to have the driver turn his back.

None of the working-class Guatemalans could mistake Lyons and Blancanales as countrymen; Lyons's blond hair and blue eyes identified him as a North American, and Blancanales, though darker, with Hispanic features and easy Spanish, did not look Guatemalan. Even though the drivers recognized the two separate North Americans as foreigners, which meant Lyons and Blancanales could not be Guatemalan police or security officers, the drivers still gave them the same cold hatred as Merida. Why? Did they mistake the North Americans for someone else?

Lyons paused, secretively keyed his hand-radio. "Pol, I do not like this. Something's happening here and I don't know what."

"Think *I* know?" Blancanales whispered.

Drivers and assistants and passengers scattered. An Indian woman waiting in a bus saw something moving below her window—her eyes widened and she dropped down out of sight. The sidewalk cleared, people shoving their friends, hurrying them away.

Lyons's pulse roared in his ears. He snapped a glance back at Blancanales, saw the ex-Green Beret already dropping to a crouch, his right hand going under his coat for his pistol. Lyons heard Gadgets's voice shout through his earphone:

"They're here! The colonel and four goons in flashy suits—"

Through the radio, he heard brakes screech. Then the frequency went to electron noise.

Lyons pulled his four-inch Colt Python from his shoulder holster and crouched with his back to the red and turquoise front of a bus. His eyes searched the area—the now deserted walkway and vendor stalls in front of him, the bus windshields and windows behind him. He eased his head past the right headlight and looked down the eighteen-inch gap between the bus and the next. Nothing moved.

Meanwhile Blancanales called Gadgets again and again. No answer. Finally:

"Carl! Where's Merida?"

"Our liaison? Probably out there with a goon squad."

Looking across the walkway, Lyons saw two Indian children watching him. Their eyes flicked back and forth, from him to a point on the left side of the bus, six feet from where Lyons crouched.

Lyons shifted the Python to his left hand. He extended his left arm. He leaned down to look under the bumper. He saw two scuffed and torn shoes behind the front wheel. Infinitely slowly, the shoes crept through the black fluid and the filth and litter in the gutter. The shoes neared the front of the bus.

The front sight and barrel of a revolver appeared around the edge of the bus at waist height. Lyons tensed, then made his move even as the shoes splashed through the gutter, the man jumping out from around the fender to shoot, only to sprawl as the North American grabbed the pistol's barrel and jerked the gunman off balance. As the man fell, Lyons whipped back his Python and backhanded the gunman with the pistol's heavy barrel.

Shots. A bullet slammed into a fender. Lyons straightened, turned, heard the quiet *rip-rip-rip* of Blancanales's silenced Beretta 93-R, the three-shot burst hammering steel and breaking glass.

"DON'T SHOOT!" Lyons screamed. "THERE'S PEOPLE AND LITTLE KIDS EVERYWHERE!"

But the other pistol fired again. Lyons felt a fist slam into his head. He struggled with the gunman who had risen up from the sidewalk, the man's right fist clubbing Lyons in the head and face and shoulder again and again.

Lyons saw who he fought. The man looked like a

beggar, his clothes ragged and patched, but he was not old. Webbed scar tissue twisted the right side of his face and hooded his sunken, blind right eye. The beggar's left hand gripped a blue-steel revolver. His right hand would never grip anything again, only knotted burn scars and stubs of fingers remaining.

Forcing the beggar's pistol to the concrete, Lyons blocked another blow from the stumpy hand and put his Python against the beggar's throat. But he did not fire. He wanted a prisoner. Lyons ended the fight by slamming his knee up into the beggar's crotch. He heard the man gasp and choke with the pain. A slug tore past Lyons's head.

Broken glass showered him, gutter slime splashed his face as he rolled off the low curb and went flat under the bus. The beggar was already gone.

Lyons crabbed under the bus, his hands sliding in the mashed vegetables and excrement and motor oil, the underside of the engine and transmission tearing at his sports coat. He paused for an instant, looking in the direction of the shots.

Two buses away, he saw expensive shoes. He recognized the fabric of the slacks. Lyons went flat on his belly in the dirt. He raised his filth-covered Python, sighted on Merida's right food, and fired.

Merida fell screaming. He rolled and thrashed in the gutter, the black slime ruining his Italian attire. Lyons crawled under the buses, found Merida's Colt Government Model .45, and eased down the hammer as the man moaned and clutched his shattered foot. Lyons put the Colt in his pocket, flipped Merida onto his face, and put the Python against the back of his head. Lyons keyed his hand-radio.

"I've got our liaison man. Where'd that beggar go?"

Gadgets's voice answered. "Move it, boys. The whole city must've heard that shoot-out."

Someone ran to Lyons. He whipped the pistol around and saw Blancanales, the silenced Beretta 93-R autopistol in his hands.

"The beggar's gone," Blancanales told him. "No one else—"

"Ironman! Pol! Move it!" Gadgets shouted through their earphones. "We've got to get out of here! I mean, now!"

Lyons looked back the way they had come. "Straight out—"

Each man grabbed one of Merida's arms and jerked him to his feet. He screamed as his weight went onto his shattered foot, then Lyons and Blancanales dragged him from the parked buses.

Drivers stared, people backed away as the three men lurched through the chaos, Lyons and Blancanales sometimes dragging Merida, sometimes carrying him. Lyons shouldered through a wall of baskets. He kicked aside panicked chickens.

Blancanales shouted out: "*Policía! Emergencia!*"

Thrashing through the hanging plastic of a booth's sunshade, Lyons stumbled over piles of avocados, mangoes and bananas. He went down in a tangle with Merida. The wounded man screamed. The fruit smashed under them. Blancanales jerked them to their feet.

Indian women ran, the bright colors of their *huipiles* flashing with instants of sunlight. Lyons pushed a child aside, stepped over another display of fruit on a tarp, dragged Merida through the bananas and mangoes. Blancanales called ahead in Spanish, warning the people.

"Alto!" A policeman shouted into their faces, his M-1 carbine levelled at them. Blancanales kicked him as Lyons chopped down on the barrel of the rifle.

The policeman fired. Lyons felt the muzzle flash, felt the bullet shock Merida as it hit the already wounded man. Lyons released Merida for an instant as he pulled the carbine from the policeman's hands and straight-armed the man aside. Blancanales carried Merida. Ten steps farther, Lyons threw the rifle onto a corrugated-steel shanty roof.

Leaving the shacks and stalls behind, they ran through brilliant sunlight. People stared as the three filthy, bloody men staggered up a hard dirt incline to the street.

A horn sounded. "Ironman! Politician!"

Weaving through buses and trucks, the Silverado's horn blaring, Gadgets drove over the curb. He braked just short of crashing into a vendor's sidewalk stall. The vendor grabbed a small child and hastily followed his wife and three other children down the dirt slope, away from the crazed North Americans.

Blancanales jerked open the side door. Lyons shoved Merida onto the second seat, then jumped in on top of him. Blancanales followed, crawling over Lyons and Merida as Gadgets threw the wagon into reverse. They bounced off the curb backward, continued swerving backward through traffic. Then Gadgets stood on the brakes, shifted gear, and accelerated.

Swerving from lane to lane, leaning on the horn, shouting out the window, Gadgets careered through the crowded streets. Blancanales crawled into the front seat. He found himself sitting on a bloody machete. He looked over to his partner, saw blood on Gadgets's hands.

"I won't ask what happened."

Gadgets detoured over a sidewalk, crashed through a pasteboard sign, then bounced off the curb. He whipped around a corner, and floored the accelerator.

"Goon squad hits the shit! Film at eleven!"

Tires screeching, Gadgets braked at a stop sign. The afternoon traffic of a major boulevard passed. Waiting for a gap in the cars and trucks and buses, Gadgets eased through a leisurely right turn, and merged with traffic.

In the back seat, Lyons checked Captain Merida's wounds. The Magnum hollowpoint had shattered his foot. Strands of flesh and tendons hung out of the exit-torn shoe. The .30-caliber slug from the policeman's carbine had gouged his ribs, but not entered his chest cavity. Blood had ruined forever the Guatemalan's Italian fashions.

Lyons looked at himself. Blood and filth and mashed fruit covered his clothes. Slime coated his Python. He heard Gadgets laughing. He looked up to see his partner watching him in the rearview mirror.

"Dig it, Ironman," Gadgets said, shaking his head. "I know all about dirty wars—but man, you stink!"

5

TRAVELING AT ONE HUNDRED KILOMETERS PER HOUR
on a freeway to the village of Amitatlan, Able Team
interrogated Captain Merida. Lyons and Blancanales
shoved their wounded prisoner down into the foot-
well between the front and second seats, and held
him down with their feet.

Gadgets drove, watching the buses and trucks and
cars in the lanes beside the Silverado for police.

Lyons stripped off his filth-ruined sports coat. He
put on a black nylon windbreaker to conceal his
shoulder-holstered Python. Blancanales asked the
questions.

"Where did you intend to take us? Blancanales
asked him.

"Why do you do this, gringos? Are you Communists?" Merida gasped.

"Where did you intend to take us?" Blancanales
repeated.

"My superiors said you search for Unomundo.
They told me to help you. But now you torture me."

"Who are your superiors?"

"Colonel Morales."

"Who else works for Unomundo?"

"We are patriots. We will save our nation from
communism."

"Answer the questions," Lyons hissed.

Blancanales continued patiently, his voice quiet and calm. "Where did you intend to take us?"

"To the buses. To find the man who worked—"

Lyons slapped the sole of Merida's shattered foot. The young officer screamed into the floormats. He thrashed and struggled to break the plastic handcuffs binding his wrists and ankles.

Blancanales glanced to the cars in the other lanes. With the windows of the Silverado rolled up and the traffic noise drowning out what sound escaped, the other drivers heard nothing. Blancanales continued his quiet interrogation.

"We know you and the colonel intended to kidnap us, then kill us. Tell us where you would have taken us."

Merida sobbed with the pain. *"Hijos de putas... comunistas... gringos comunistas..."*

"Don't call us Communists," Lyons told him. He emphasized his next words with taps to the prisoner's shattered foot. "Answer—" Tap. "—the—" Tap. "—question." Tap.

Merida arched back with agony at each word. Slamming his forehead into the floormat again and again, he tried to beat himself unconscious. Blancanales put his foot on the back of Merida's neck to immobilize him.

"Answer the questions, cooperate with us, and you live. If you do not, you will suffer terribly, then die. Your officers and friends, your family will never know of your courage and sacrifice. They will never find your body. We will tell them we paid you money, flew you to Miami to start a new life. They will remember you as a traitor. Perhaps your family will suffer. If you cooperate, we will arrange that you can say you escaped from us. You will have your pride, you can tell the others of your courage, you can live to see your children have children. Answer the questions and you live."

His breath still coming in ragged sobs, Merida considered the offer. Finally he told them:

"It is too late for you. You cannot stop Unomundo now. We will take Guatemala. We will liberate our country from the Communists and the Indians and the Jews and the scum of mixed races. Whether I live or die, the future is ours, for we are strong and pure."

His monologue silenced Able Team. Lyons and Blancanales only stared at their prisoner. Gadgets spoke first.

"You know what that sounds like? *Sieg Heil*."

"You low-life Nazi scum hole," Lyons cursed. "Pol, give me your Beretta. I'm going to make this world a better place to live."

"No. I gave my word. If he cooperates, he lives."

"I didn't give my word. What's it going to be, you petty pompous Nazi? Dachaus for the Indians? A Holocaust? What makes you so strong and pure and perfect? Because you look European? Because you speak Spanish? Because you have money and wear a suit? I'm the strong one now, and I'm purifying the earth of you—"

Lyons put his Python against the back of Merida's head and thumbed back the hammer. Captain Merida heard the hammer lock back. He twisted and sobbed, looked up at Blancanales.

"I will tell you! Colonel Morales is my commander. He speaks with Unomundo. He will take you to Unomundo. I have the address of our meeting place."

"You will take us there?"

"Yes, yes. Now."

Blancanales smiled to Lyons, who wrote down the address that their gasping prisoner offered.

As they returned to the metropolitan center of Guatemala City, Lyons wadded his ruined sports coat and put it over Merida's ears to prevent their prisoner from hearing their words. He used a roll of two-inch-wide adhesive tape to secure the wadded coat over Merida's ears. More tape covered his eyes. Another wrap of tape covered his mouth.

Then Able Team had a whispered conference.

"The goons see this truck show up at the colonel's," Lyons told his partners, "and they'll waste us on sight."

Blancanales agreed. "We'll rent another car."

"What about this Nazi here?" Gadgets asked. "Can't drive him around the city. Anybody sees him and we're in jail. Unless maybe we rent an ambulance."

Lyons nodded. "He's a problem. I don't even trust him to take us to the colonel. Could pull some trick. If I had my way...." Lyons made a thumbs-down.

"I gave my word he'd live," Blancanales told them. "We'll leave him in the truck."

On an avenue of delicatessens and tourist shops, they spotted a car-rental agency. Gadgets stopped the Silverado in a driveway around the corner. Blancanales stepped out. He went to rent a car while Lyons and Gadgets waited.

Rush-hour traffic jammed the boulevard. Neither Gadgets nor Lyons spoke, not wanting to risk saying something that Merida might hear and later report.

Traffic passed in surges on the one-way boulevard. When a traffic light a block behind them changed, the two-cycle popping of motorbikes rose to a deafening whine, the teenagers jerking through the gears to gain the lead, shooting past in a crescendo of noise, followed a second later by a curb-to-curb wall of bumpers as trucks and cars and bumpers raced to the next red light. Motorbikes swerved in and out through the pack as more teenagers attempted to gain the forefront.

Auto exhaust brought an early dusk. The lights and neon of shops came on one at a time. Flashing signs advertised North American jeans, European watches, Japanese stereos and cameras. Only a few Mayan names on signs and the low-rise architecture distinguished the boulevard from downtown Los Angeles or a Hispanic ghetto in New York.

A Volkswagen van pulled up beside the Silverado. Blancanales honked the horn and waved. Gadgets followed the van into traffic. Ten minutes later, they parked in a quiet suburb of modest apartments and tree-shaded streets.

To give them time before Merida freed himself or beat on the inside of the abandoned Silverado to get a passerby's help, Blancanales sedated him with a shot of morphine from his med-kit. Then they transferred their packs and case-concealed weapons to the Volkswagen.

Only after they had put distance behind them did they finally speak,

"So what's our transmitter telling us about the colonel?" Gadgets asked Blancanales, who drove.

"I get sounds once in a while, voices—"

"Yeah, range fade. We're moving in and out of range."

"They're looking for us. They've got all their men out."

"What about police?" Lyons asked.

Blancanales shook his head. "These characters are not official."

"What about a false crime report, just to get us off the streets?"

"False?" Blancanales asked his ex-LAPD partner, incredulous. "Four dead men, a kidnapping, auto theft, illegal weapons, forged papers? We're a three-man crime wave, my friend. No, from the bits and pieces I've heard, there are no police, no security services, no army involved."

"Great liaison connections the Feds made for us," Lyons laughed. "Delivered us straight to a gang of Guatemalan Nazis. Next time I make my own reservations."

"Who says they're Guatemalan?" Gadgets asked. "Morales and Merida met us at the airport. There was no one else in the hangar, they had their own man at the guard post, they took us in a slow circle until their death squad was ready to take us. They could be anyone from anywhere."

"They've got some kind of official connection," Lyons responded. "When Merida kicked that old man around, he was flashing a badge to keep the crowd back. I saw an official card.''

Gadgets laughed. ''Hey, Politician. How many sets of official cards do *we* have?''

Blancanales shook his head in disagreement. ''Those bus drivers at the terminal, they recognized Merida as a hardman cop. And they thought we were cops, too.''

''No,'' Lyons said, ''it was something else, don't know what. Everyone thought I was a tourist until they saw me with Merida. Wizard, you said four goons came at you. What did they look like? What happened?''

''Four big dudes. Dark hair, tailored suits. They came to get me, but I got them. A Beretta 93-R makes a great urban equalizer. Three of them didn't know what hit them. The fourth one had on a Kevlar vest. He got in a swing with a machete. But he should've worn his Kevlar hat, too. Then I put a burst into the colonel's car as he beat it. Pol, you hear him complain of any upper-body discomfort? Maybe like a nine-millimeter headache?''

''No points, Schwarz,'' Blancanales smiled. ''You missed.''

''Bullshit! Had him dead in my sights, double-hand grip. Glass must've deflected the slugs.''

''You tried a through-the-windshield shot with nine millimeter?'' Lyons asked. ''Why'd you bother? Windshields will deflect even 5.56 military rounds.''

''It was the back windshield. Tempered glass. The nines broke it. I knew the first one would go wild, but I thought number two and three might score. Konzaki's custom steel cores and all that jazz.''

"Nine millimeter was designed to kill Europeans," Lyons told them. "For dangerous people, you got to use .45 caliber."

They laughed at Lyons's cynicism. Blancanales finally reminded them of the task at hand. "Gentlemen, if I can have your attention. We're looking for an address."

Using a tourist map from the car-rental agency, Able Team drove through the streets and boulevards of the central city. Blancanales had no difficulty with the traffic, but few of the corners had streets signs. One-way streets forced him to drive past certain streets and then circle back. At last they found the correct avenue, and cruised slowly down the block, reading the numbers.

They found the number on a café's window. Looking in at the patrons and waitresses, Lyons shook his head.

"That Nazi tricked us."

"What do these big numbers on the map mean?" Gadgets asked Blancanales.

"What numbers?"

"These." Gadgets pointed out several faint numbers with penlight.

They saw large numbers in faint blue ink superimposed over the streets and rivers of Guatemala City. The number 1 marked the old center of the city. The number 9 marked the area of the international airport. The number 19 marked a suburb ten miles away.

Blancanales drove to the corner and looked at the street sign. The sign read, 6 AVENIDA Z. 1.

"Zones! The city's divided into zones."

"That Nazi Merida didn't give us the zone number!" Lyons cursed. "I told you. He fooled us."

"If you remember," Blancanales reminded Lyons, "he had your Python up against his skull. Tricking us was not his number one concern. He just forgot to give us the zone."

"How many zones? Nineteen?" Lyons groaned with frustration. "We're going to spend the night driving in circles."

A taxi passed the parked Volkswagen. Blancanales turned to his partners. "Carl, you're going to be a lost tourist. Give the address to a cab driver. We'll have a microphone on you. We'll follow the cab. The driver will know what zones have this kind of address. You just keep saying, 'No, that's not the place.' We'll go back later and check out the most likely places."

"All right, makes sense. And just in case they find us first. . . ." Lyons grabbed the fiberboard case concealing his Atchisson as he stepped into the cool evening air. Gadgets called out:

"Remember, be discreet."

Lyons stood at the curb in his black windbreaker and filth-spotted slacks, holding the guitar case. Farther down from the intersection, the nightlife of the Guatemalan capital already sparkled. Neon flashed, music blared from cars, teenagers walked arm-in-arm. As he walked, Lyons came across what looked like a shop-front casino; inside, young men crowded around a video game. They cheered their friend when he won, the machine paying off like a slot machine, tokens spilling onto the floor. As Lyons stared around him, Guatemalans stared at him, smiled when he met their eyes. He looked at himself in a shop window and laughed. *I look just like an ex-cop on a rock-n-roll tour of Guatemala*.

A taxi slowed, the driver motioning to Lyons. Lyons stepped from the curb and got in the back. A young driver with a prematurely lined face greeted him in perfect English.

"Good evening, sir. Where would you like to go?"

Lyons gave him the address, then commented: "Your English is better than mine. You go to school up north?"

"Yes, sir, several years." The young driver spoke in a quiet, forlorn tone. "Have you been in Guatemala long, sir?"

"Only today." Lyons watched the crowded sidewalks and bright shops flash past as the driver eased through traffic.

"Will you be staying long, sir?"

"No, just here on business. Get it done, go home. But I think I'll come back on my own time one of these days. On the flight down, I looked at a lot of pictures of the Indians. Their weaving. Their villages. The mountains. All I've seen so far is the city. But maybe my business will take me into the mountains."

"Yes, sir. The mountains are beautiful."

The driver swept through a smooth right-hand turn. Lyons felt the taxi slow. To the left, he saw a park lit with soft amber streetlamps. Lovers strolled the walkways, children ran through the night-shadows. Families crowded around vendors selling roast corn-on-the-cob, steaks, tacos, candies.

The taxi's curbside door opened and a man took the seat next to him even as Lyons jerked his Python from under his windbreaker and pointed it at the horribly burned, one-eyed young beggar.

His scars twisting with a smile, the beggar held up his left hand, palm open, empty. Like the taxi driver, he also spoke perfect English.

"Tell me, sir. What business do you have with Colonel Morales?"

6

WITH THE MUZZLE OF CARL LYON'S PYTHON against his heart, the disfigured beggar introduced himself.

"I am Dr. Orozco. We—" his one eye looked to the cab driver "—are enemies of Unomundo. Is it true that you three men have come to Guatemala to fight Unomundo?"

"You tried to shoot me at the bus station. Why?" Lyons demanded, knowing the mini-mike in his jacket pocket transmitted his words to his partners. He looked out the back window and saw the Volkswagen tailgating the taxi. Gadgets had the side window down, and his hands were out of sight below the dashboard.

"That was a misunderstanding. I intended to kill Merida. He was one of those who did this to me." The man touched his hideously scarred face with the fingerless lump of his right hand.

Glancing outside to the crowded plaza, the scarred doctor took a soft cap from his pocket. He put it on his head and pulled it down to shadow the right side of his face.

"Please put the pistol away. If you shoot me here.... There is the National Palace—the President's offices, guarded by the elite of our country's commandos. On the other side, the headquarters of the National Police. There are sharpshooters and secret police guarding the president's offices and the police buildings every moment of the day and night. If I die, you will live only a minute longer."

Lyons realized that they had kept to the plaza since Dr. Orozco entered the taxi. The driver made only left turns, stopping for signals, slowing for crowded crosswalks and jaywalking soldiers, but never leaving the rectangle of four wide boulevards.

"Very smooth," Lyons admitted. But he did not holster the revolver. He covered it with his wind-breaker.

The doctor continued. "Though I always instruct my friends to be patient, to live with their anger and hatred, to discpline their emotions, I failed to follow my own preaching. I—" He thought of the correct word in United States English. "I snapped. It was fortunate that you stopped me."

Lyons smiled slightly. "Not too fortunate for your head. Or your balls."

"Pain is relative. The cuts and bruises you inflicted will heal in only a few days. In my rage, I did not even see you. If you had been one of Unomundo's mercenaries, I would again be Merida's prisoner. My previous experience with Merida was very bad. I could only expect worse on the second experience. Please, you avoided my question. Did you come to Guatemala to fight Unomundo?"

The hand-radio that was clipped to Lyons's belt buzzed. He keyed it with his left hand. He asked his partners, "What do you think?"

Blancanales's voice answered. "Ask Dr. Orozco to join us in this car. We'll talk."

The scar-faced man nodded. "Certainly. Luis, we can leave the park now."

The driver turned right, the Volkswagen on his bumper, and proceeded down an avenue until he turned right onto a dark side street. Blancanales parked behind them.

The two passengers left the taxi. Lyons, his Python held ready under his windbreaker, saw headlights swing around the corner and stop. He looked in the other direction and saw a motorbike swerve into the shadows. Its headlight went black, but the rider did not dismount.

"You people are organized," Lyons muttered as he opened the Volskwagen's sliding door. He got in. Dr. Orozco followed him.

Gadgets winced at the doctor's scars, found he had to look away. The doctor ignored the North American's shock and extended his left hand for handshakes.

"It is a pleasure to meet you, gentlemen. And now that I can speak with all of you, let us discuss fighting Unomundo together."

"How do you know what we're here for?" Lyons asked.

"After you abandoned Captain Merida, we questioned him."

"You've followed us all day?" Gadgets asked, amazed.

"We thought your escape from the terminal very dramatic. Very much like American television."

"Who do you represent?" Blancanales asked.

"I represent our group. We have talked together and agreed to help you."

"What are your politics?" Lyons demanded.

Dr. Orozco smiled. "You Yankees are so naive. First, if we were Communists, would I tell you? And if we were, would you now be alive? Do not judge us all by the bumbling of a one-handed, half-blind doctor stupid with the thought of revenge. We have grenades, we have machine guns. We could have killed you a hundred times today."

"You have any foreign connections?" Lyons asked.

"You mean, Russia? Libya? Nicaragua? No. We have families and friends in the United States and Mexico and Europe. Sometimes they send us money. But we do not need it. We work."

Blancanales asked next. "Are you in opposition to the present government?"

"The new president is a gift from God. When he came to office, our group disbanded, only to learn that Unomundo and the other fascists who had escaped justice still threatened our country. Now, with the elections only weeks away, the threat is at its greatest. Unomundo has spies in the government and the army. We do not know what he plans, but it will come soon. To fight Unomundo, you need our help. And though it shames me to ask, we need the help of the United States."

"How long have you known of Unomundo?" Blancanales asked.

"Since this...." He touched the scarred right half of his face with what remained of his right hand. "Only a few months out of school. For my church, I volunteered to work in a clinic for Indians. I gave a wounded man first aid and called for an ambulance.

Merida came with a squad of killers. They wanted the names of the others fighting Unomundo. But I knew no names. They beat me, they put my hand in a fire. I knew no names. They put my face to the fire. I knew no names. They threw me in a ditch, shot me, buried me. But I lived. That was when I learned of Unomundo."

The North Americans said nothing. In the silence of the car, they heard the traffic sounds of the boulevards, and a woman singing. Gadgets shook his head, sighed quietly: "Nazis...."

"Will you help us in our fight?" Dr. Orozco asked.

The men of Able Team looked to one another. They nodded.

"Good," beamed the disfigured young man. "We help each other. After you took Merida, the Nazis evacuated those offices. But we followed them to another place. Luis, that man—" Dr. Orozco pointed to the cab driver waiting in the taxi "—he will guide you. When I learned of an American commando team attacking Unomundo, I mobilized all our people. We will stop the fascists. We must. God be with you."

Dr. Orozco stepped out of the van and raised his hand to signal the car parked at the far end of the block. The tires burned rubber as the driver roared to the van. In five seconds, the disfigured young doctor was gone.

Gadgets broke the silence. "One brave hombre. That happens to him and he still plays the game."

"No," Lyons corrected. "He wasn't in any game. They just did it."

"Talk about gifts from God," Blancanales added. "Dr. Orozco and his people are a gift to us. I feel it about this guy. From the evidence on his face, I kinda trust his story."

"Unomundo's got to go." Gadgets eased down the hammer of his Beretta 93-R. He set the safety. He returned the autopistol to his shoulder holster. "Got... To...Go."

"First, we got to find him," Lyons said as he reached into his war bag heavy with steel. He took out the re-engineered Colt Government Model. He checked the chamber and checked the Allen screw securing the suppressor. Redesigned and hand-machined by Andrzej Konzaki to incorporate the innovations of the Beretta autopistols, the interior mechanisms of the Colt no longer resembled what Browning had invented and patented. Like the Berettas, a fold-down lever and oversized trigger guard provided a positive two-hand grip. But it fired silent full-powered .45-caliber slugs, in semi-auto and three-shot bursts. Lyons jammed in an extended ten-shot magazine, with the chamber left empty. Returning the weapon to the flight bag, Lyons gave his partners a salute: He would go with Luis and they would follow him.

"Find and kill," he said.

A few steps took him to the waiting taxi. Inside, the sallow-faced young driver turned to him. Lyons extended his hand. "We're working together, Luis. We'll break those Nazis."

The driver smiled and shook the North American's hand.

Speeding to find Colonel Morales, the taxi traveled

the brightly lit boulevard again. Lyons saw Luis glance to a crowd of laughing young men and women emerging from a restaurant. Then came a bride in flowing white and a young groom in a tuxedo. The crowd of friends showered the newlyweds with rice until they gained the shelter of the limousine.

Luis stared at the scene with longing and sorrow. For that moment, Lyons studied the young man's old face. Lyons had already heard Dr. Orozco's horror. What had Luis suffered?

LOOKING DOWN THROUGH A DIRTY SKYLIGHT, they saw Colonel Morales. The colonel supervised a crew of workers packing what appeared to be clay inside the door panels of three cars—a battered Fiat, a gleaming black Mercedes, and a blue-and-white National Police squad car. Elsewhere in the warehouse, workers packed the clay into commmonplace street objects: trash cans, striped street barricades, the underside of fiberglass park benches.

Blancanales leaned to Lyons and Luis. He pointed to a shipping crate, then motioned to all the objects the workers packed. "That's C-4. Plastic explosive."

"They are making bombs?" Luis asked.

Lyons nodded. He slipped back from the skylight to key his hand-radio. He whispered to Gadgets.

"Guess what? It's a bomb factory. Car bombs, booby traps. Enough to make this city Beirut-for-a-day. What's going on out front?"

"*Nada*, man. Zero. Guard number one's got a cigar in the car. Guard number two's asleep on his feet."

"The doctor's people in position?"

"First shot they hear, it's blacktop kill zone."

"Stand by. Over."

Blancanales snapped his fingers to get Lyons's attention. He pointed down. "Two guards coming up," he hissed.

Lyons went to the stairwell housing, moving as quickly as he dared over the sun-cracked tar of the warehouse roof.

He felt the footsteps on the stairs before he heard them. Pressing his back against the housing, he thumbed back his silent Colt's hammer and waited.

Voices. Sentries. The door swung open, light fanning across the dark rooftop. Lyons saw one man with a folded-stock Galil autorifle in his hands. The man called out.

A second man looked around the corner, his eyes going wide as he looked straight into Lyons's face.

Grabbing the guy by the hair, Lyons jerked the sentry's face into the muzzle of the silent Colt, and pulled the trigger twice.

He tried to shove the dead man away, but stumbled over the corpse. Still he aimed one-handed at the other sentry, and fired.

The slug clanged off the Galil's barrel and tore through the man's right bicep. The guy sucked down a breath as the pain came, but the scream never left his throat, a second .45-caliber hollowpoint punching into his chest. The third went high, tearing away the top of his head.

Lyons changed magazines. On one knee he listened for an alarm. The roof door swung back and forth on its hinges, and voices came from below; a worker used a power drill. But he heard no shouting, no rush of feet on the stairs.

He looked over to Blancanales. His partner gave him a thumbs-up, then he and Luis crept across to join Lyons. They stripped the Galils from the dead men. They found 9mm automatics in shoulder holsters. Lyons nudged Luis.

"Put on that one's coat, and sling the rifle over your shoulder. Pol, you make like the other man. Down the stairs, left into the office. I want that phony colonel alive."

Descending the stairs, Luis and Blancanales screened Lyons with their bodies. They watched the floor of the warehouse. The workers continued in their preparation for the death and dismemberment of thousands of innocent people. Colonel Morales helped a worker press a sheet of C-4 into a wide flat box. Then another worker poured thousands of steel nuts and bolts over the plastic explosive to fill the box. They closed the box, and taped it tight to create a one-foot-by-two-foot Claymore mine.

The three invaders cut from the stairs to the door of the windowless office. Blancanales watched a worker pasting newspaper over the improvised Claymore. The bomb would be placed at a newsstand, to spray an intersection or an entire city block with crude but deadly shrapnel. Lyons, now in front of the "sentries," pushed open the door. He saw a young man leaning over a map of Guatemala City. The man spoke without looking up.

"Coronel. Aquí está la otra—"

A silent .45 slug through the top of the head rocked him back. His arms flailed like a spastic marionette before he collapsed to the floor. Already dead, his last breath wheezed through blood in his throat.

Pointing to the telephone, Lyons whispered to Luis: "Can you get that phone to ring? Call somebody, get them to call you back?"

Luis nodded. He dialed the operator. *"Señorita. Hay una problema con este teléfono. Es posible...."*

Lyons and Blancanales watched the interior of the warehouse through cracks in the wood of the office wall. Beside them, the phone rang, once, twice, three times.

Finally, Colonel Morales looked toward the ringing telephone. He called out: "Armando! Armando!"

When the ringing continued, the colonel marched to the office.

Once inside, Blancanales pinned his arms. Lyons slapped a hand over his mouth and asked. "You want to live, Nazi? Want to live?"

Seeing Lyons's face, the colonel threw himself back, twisting and kicking. But Blancanales and Luis wrestled him to his knees. Lyons felt the colonel gasping against his palm as he put his knee into the middle-aged man's back to immobilize him. Making sure the guy had seen the silenced Colt, Lyons pressed the weapon to the back of the colonel's head.

"I want to hear you say you want to live. Say it."

"Traitor to your race!" the colonel grunted.

Lyons hooked his elbow around the colonel's throat and jerked his head back. He kicked his prisoner's knees apart from behind, and hissed:

"You're a brave one, Nazi. You think you're a

man because you torture and murder. But are you brave enough to learn a new word? The word is eunuch...."

He jammed the muzzle of the auto-Colt up between the colonel's legs.

The colonel went white. A whine rattled in his throat. Watching, Luis laughed. Lyons looked to the young man. Luis enjoyed the fear and suffering of the officer.

"Shoot him, American! It will be justice."

Lyons ignored the laughter and the demand for revenge. He continued the interrogation of the man he held.

"Now, do you cooperate? Tell me, Nazi!"

"Yes, yes, I—"

"Shout that the police are coming. The army. Tell your scum terrorist crew to run. Now! Shout it!"

Shouting out in Spanish, the colonel told his workers to evacuate the warehouse.

They called out to him, he told them to flee. He would follow soon in a moment.

Blancanales keyed his hand-radio to alert Gadgets. "Nazis coming out. Hit them all."

From his position on a rooftop across the street, Gadgets sighted his silenced Heckler & Koch MP-5SD3 submachine gun, the electronics of the Starlite scope illuminating the shadowy doorway of the warehouse. He snapped single shots into the chest of every green-glowing form that left through the door.

In the office, Lyons jerked Colonel Morales to his feet. "Okay, Nazi. Now you take us to Unomundo."

The colonel's eyes rolled in panic. "*Pero no sé....*

I do not know. He is in the mountains. I see him only at meetings."

"How do you communicate?"

"Sometimes telephone, sometimes couriers."

"Take us to the couriers."

7

TWO SOLDIERS GUARDED THE IRON GATES of the estate. The teenagers in camouflage and combat gear looked at the taxi as it passed by the street. Seeing only a cab driver and a blond North American, the soldiers returned to throwing coins against the guard post's wall.

Lyons looked back. Within the wide gates, a long, lighted driveway crossed an immaculate lawn. The glare of floodlights around the mansion created an all-night noon. Mercury-arc security lights bathed the landscaping and garages behind the big house.

A spiked iron fence, eight feet high and topped with concertina wire, enclosed the estate. As the taxi cruised past, dogs ran along the fence. Dogs barked from adjoining estates. But Lyons saw no sentries at the other gates on the avenue. He keyed his hand-radio.

"It's a high-security mansion. It's got dogs. Lights. Razor wire. Two soldiers out front. This Lieutenant Garcia lives real well on army pay."

Questioning Colonel Morales, Able Team had learned the identities and duties of Lieutenant Garcia and his wife. Both served Unomundo as couriers. Garcia exploited his post in the Office of Army Intelligence to maintain contacts with other traitors in

the army and government. Señora Garcia, a co-
ordinator in the Department of Tourism, traveled
throughout the nation to arrange Indian cere-
monies and markets for tourists. She carried information to and from Unomundo's base in the
mountains.

"Think we can go straight in?" Blancanales asked
Lyons by radio.

"Three possibilities. A tunnel. Or parachutes. Or
straight through the gate. I think I can take them
quiet. There's no one else on the street to see it happen. You got any alcohol?"

"Huh?"

"Rubbing alcohol. In your medical kit."

"Come and get it."

"There in a minute."

Luis had listened to the radio conference. "You
will kill the soldiers? With that silent gun?"

Lyons shook his head. "We don't know that
they're Nazis. They look like eighteen-year-old
draftees pulling guard duty."

"You must kill them. It is the only way. Any alarm
will bring many trucks of soldiers."

"No. Why should they die for other people's
politics?"

A few blocks away, Gadgets and Blancanales
waited in the rented van, the Nazi colonel tied and
gagged on the floor. Within sight of the North
Americans, three other cars waited. Squads of men
and women from Dr. Orozco's anti-fascist group
watched for a signal from Blancanales. They all had
good weapons now, snatched from the dead Nazis
after the ambush on the bomb factory.

As the taxi slowed beside the van, Blancanales extended his arm from the window and said to Lyons:

"If there's trouble, we're thirty seconds away. Good luck."

"Won't be any trouble." Lyons took the plastic bottle. As the taxi returned to the avenue of the wealthy, Lyons splashed the alcohol on his shirt and jacket. Then he scribbled an illegible series of numbers and names on a scrap of paper.

"Let me out at the corner," he said.

Luis turned to Lyons and spoke with sneering hatred. "Kill them. They would not hesitate to kill you."

"That makes it exciting," Lyons laughed.

Stumbling from the taxi, he fell. He wobbled to his feet. He almost fell again as he slammed the door closed. Luis accelerated away, leaving Lyons alone on the avenue.

Glancing at the scrap of paper, Lyons staggered down the center of the avenue. He stopped from time to time to look for address numbers. Finally, he walked to the soldiers.

The teenagers watched the drunken North American. Laughing, they motioned him away. Lyons held up the paper.

"This is where my friends are." He pointed at the paper, then pointed at the house.

"*Lo siento, gringo. No hablo inglés. Vayase, por favor.*"

"Really, guys. They invited me to a party. Here's the address."

The teenage soldiers smelled the alcohol as Lyons approached. Still laughing, one of the soldiers took the paper. While he tried to read the scrawl, Lyons staggered to the gate. Gripping the bars, weaving on his feet, he scanned the grounds. No other soldiers guarded the estate.

"Señor, no se permiten a—"

Driving a kick into the nearest boy's stomach, Lyons dropped him instantly. As the other teenager grabbed for the pistol grip of his Galil, Lyons simultaneously kneed him in the groin and smashed an elbow against the underside of his jaw. The youth tumbled. The first boy groaned on the ground. Using his right fist like a hammer, Lyons smashed down on the back of the boy's head, stunning him.

He took their rifles, then dragged them into the guard booth. Jerking plastic handcuffs around their wrists, he searched their pockets for the gate keys. Lyons buzzed Blancanales and Gadgets.

"Come on in. But only bring one carload of our friends. Could look very suspicious if—"

"My thoughts exactly," Gadgets answered. "There in a second."

Headlights flashed. Lyons pressed himself into the darkness of the shadows. He saw the plastic dome-light of the taxi.

Luis parked in the entryway, the doors of the taxi only a step from the guard post.

They loaded the teenage soldiers into the taxi, then opened the gate. Seconds later, the rented van and a late-model Fiat sedan followed the taxi into the estate.

His silenced Colt in his hand, Lyons ran to the front door. He heard the others rushing from the cars as he sighted on the lock, fired twice, and kicked the door open.

Standing in a white entryway decorated with European pop art, a slender young woman in a form-hugging gown of red acetate screamed. Behind her, a mustached man in a tuxedo and bow tie dropped to one knee, his hands going for a pistol in an ankle holster.

Lyons leaped in, straight-armed the woman in the throat, her scream stopping as if switched off, then sprinted three steps to the man and kicked him in the face. The man rolled back, blood spraying from his smashed nose, a small pistol flying from his hand.

Blancanales held and questioned the two while Luis searched through the desk drawers and file cabinets of the lieutenant's office. Lyons and the squad of anti-fascist fighters swept through the house. In the bedrooms, they found an elderly nanny and two children.

"They don't know the exact location of the base," Blancanales told Lyons and Gadgets when they reunited. "Lieutenant Garcia never goes into the mountains. The señora only goes as far as a village at the end of the paved road, a place called Azatlan. From there, she says, Unomundo's men or local policemen take the information."

Lyons squatted in front of the handcuffed couple. Tears streamed down the woman's face, powder and mascara splattering on her breasts. The lieutenant glared hate at the North American who had broken his nose.

"Why the bombs?" Lyons asked them.

The woman glanced to her husband. He shook his head. They did not answer.

"I asked you, why the bombs?"

Luis rushed from the lieutenant's office, sheets of typed columns in his hands. "Look. These are death lists. Every name a corpse. Or a family butchered. She has murdered hundreds of—"

"No! I killed no one. I only carry messages. I am a courier."

The three North Americans checked the typed sheets. A penciled *X* marked most of the names. Lyons smiled to the woman.

"Tonight you carry another message to Azatlan. Us."

"No! No! *Por el amor de Dios*," Señora Garcia cried out. "Unomundo will kill us. Kill my babies."

"You will take them to the Nazis," Luis told her, "or *we* will kill your children."

Blancanales motioned Lyons and Gadgets to one side. Keeping their voices low, they discussed their options.

"If we take her with us," Blancanales suggested, "she could lead us directly to her contact. With these people holding her husband and children, she won't give us any problems."

"I don't want to take the doctor's squads with us," Lyons whispered. "Carloads of people with rifles and pistols get noticed."

"Yeah, and we don't have the extra radios," Gadgets added. "Mucho problems with communications."

"That, too," Lyons agreed. "But the fact is, I don't trust them. That Luis, we don't take him in for the hit, okay?"

"You're paranoid," Gadgets said.

Blancanales agreed. "He's proved himself. He doesn't work for Unomundo."

"That's not it. Luis is twisted. Something happened to him. All he wants to do is kill and torture—"

Gadgets laughed. "The Ironman doesn't like that?"

"I do what is necessary. I don't enjoy it. You know that."

Blancanales cut off the talk. "We'll take her to Azatlan to make the contact. We'll take Luis with us so he can bring the woman back immediately. Agreed?"

They nodded. The anti-fascist fighters took the lieutenant and the children away in a car. Señora Garcia's face was a mask of grief and panic as her family disappeared. Other fighters loaded the lieutenant's files into another car. Luis reported to Able Team.

"My people will hold the traitor and his children until we return. The death lists and messages from Unomundo will go to the newspapers after we break the fascists. How many fighters do you need for the attack?"

"None," Lyons told him. "Your fighters can shoot, but they aren't trained soldiers."

"Three men? Against many soldiers and mercenaries?"

"We only need to kill one man," Lyons answered. "Unomundo."

IN TWO CARS—the rented Volkswagen van and Lieutenant Garcia's unmarked Dodge—Able Team traveled west, following the Pan American Highway through the foothills and ravines surrounding Guatemala City. Traffic was moderate. Luis, wearing tailored and pressed fatigues from the lieutenant's wardrobe, drove for Lyons and Señora Garcia. Blancanales and Gadgets followed in the Volkswagen.

Switching on an official-band radio in the Dodge, they heard military and police units reporting on the massacre in front of the warehouse. Luis translated for Lyons.

"They call them Communist terrorists... fourteen dead... no weapons, but some of the dead men had holsters for pistols... it is now being investigated by the army...."

Lyons keyed his hand-radio to brief Blancanales and Gadgets.

"We're monitoring the police units at the bomb factory. The police have turned it over to the army to investigate. Seems they think it was a Communist terror operation."

"What about Colonel Morales?" Blancanales asked.

"Nothing.

"...they have no witnesses...."

"Anything about three North Americans?"

"Nothing yet."

Luis continued to translate as he followed the winding freeway through the night. "...there is another report... an army colonel murdered by guerillas on the highway... Colonel Crespo."

"You know this Crespo?" Lyons asked.

"Did you take his name to Unomundo?" Luis demanded of Señora Garcia, who rode silently in the back seat, her hands cuffed behind her, plastic hand-cuffs looped around her ankles. "Answer me!"

But she only cried. Luis cursed her in Spanish. He told Lyons: "The president appointed him to reform the National Police. Colonel Crespo threw out those who kidnapped and tortured and murdered. And now he is dead, machinegunned in Chimaltenango. By *hombres desconocidos*. Unknown men. It was unknown men who killed my wife and baby. Are you proud of that, *puta*? *Puta fascista*?"

"I killed no one. My husband killed no one."

Luis flashed a glance of hatred at the woman in the back seat. "You think your lies will save you? I saw the lists! I know—"

He went quiet to listen to the military-police radio. "Roadblock! They will search cars for the Communists."

"Where?"

He pointed ahead.

"Pol. Wizard. We got problems. We're going into a roadblock."

"Any way to go around it?" Gadgets asked.

Luis heard the question from the hand-radio. "Tell your friends I have the fascist's identification. In this uniform and this automobile, perhaps they will allow us to pass without a search."

"With a foreigner and a woman?" Lyons asked. "And what about my partners?"

"Well. . . perhaps we will pass before they close the highway."

Accelerating, they swerved through the late-night traffic. The powerful Dodge passed the other cars easily, flashing past buses and trucks laboring up the incline. But the Volkswagen lagged. The hand-radio buzzed.

"Ironman!" Gadgets called. "We can't keep up. This thing's got a small engine—"

"Forget it. We're there."

Traffic jammed bumper-to-bumper in the lanes, clouds of exhaust glowing red with brake lights. Luis moved over the center dividing line.

"Don't try to turn around!" Lyons warned him. "They'll spot us for sure. We've got to chance it."

"Of course. But any army officer would not wait with the other cars. Radio your partners to follow."

Lyons keyed his hand-radio. "Stay on our bumper. Luis is going to the head of the line."

"Loading, locking," Gadgets answered.

"Don't even think it. Four pistols and rifles against the army?"

"If it's Unomundo's goons up there," Gadgets asked him, "do you want to be captured?"

"Loading, locking," Lyons responded, clicking off his hand-radio. He opened the Atchisson's case. He jerked back the actuator to feed the first shell into the chamber. He left the autoshotgun concealed in the unlocked case.

Luis turned to the woman. "Hear me, *puta*. You will not betray us. If we do not return to the city, your children die."

Lyons looked to the hate-filled young man. He shook his head, no. Luis laughed. He leaned on the horn as he sped past the waiting cars, flicking his high beams to warn oncoming traffic.

Troops watched from olive drab 6 x 6 trucks. Sol-

diers with autorifles went into buses and waved flashlights over the passengers. Other soldiers looked into
cars, told drivers to open their trunks. As Luis raced
to the roadblock, the soldiers in the trucks raised
their rifles.

As he slowed, Luis extended Lieutenant Garcia's
identification. A soldier put a flashlight on the
wallet, then on Lyons and Señora Garcia. An officer
came running to their car.

Lyons's right hand reached toward the Atchisson's
pistolgrip.

The officer glanced at the stolen identification and
saluted Luis. Then he looked into the car. He saw the
fair-skinned Lyons. The officer saluted again. *"Viva
Unomundo."*

Luis spoke to the officer in Spanish. The officer
looked at the two North Americans in the Volkswagen behind. Then he waved both cars past.

As they accelerated away, Luis passed the wallet to
Lyons. One plastic divider held Lieutenant Garcia's
army identification. A second held an embossed
business card. The engraved lettering said only:

"UNO, s.a."

"That means," Luis told him. "UNO, Incorporat-
ed."

"This is bad news. His people are everywhere."

Luis nodded. "Everywhere."

8

FOLLOWING THE PAN AMERICAN HIGHWAY, they drove into the high central plateau of Guatemala. A starlit landscape of shadowy mountains and black stands of forest extended into the distance. Few vehicles traveled the highway. Opening his window, Lyons put his face into the windrush. The night smelled of pines and dust and wood fires. He thought of the High Sierras of California.

They passed villages bright with lights, electric incandescence creating islands of whitewashed houses, tiled roofs, and dusty rock-paved streets. Other times, as they rounded curves, their headlights revealed fields of tangled dry cornstalks and fire-blackened adobe walls.

"What happened at these farms?" Lyons asked Luis.

"The EGP. *El Ejercito Guerilla de los Pobres*. The Guerilla Army of the Poor. They needed money for the revolution. They demanded taxes. But the farmers are without money. They have only corn and beans. When the farmers would not pay the war taxes, the guerillas took men from every family and killed them.

"When guerillas came again and demanded taxes, the people paid the few coins they had. I knew one woman, an Indian woman. The EGP killed her father and her husband, so she paid the tax to stop them killing her son.

"It was not guerillas she paid. They were agents of the *desconocidos*. The unknown men. A gang of the *desconocidos* came, raped her, then hacked her to death with machetes. They carved a hammer and sickle on her face as a warning to the other Communists.

"It happened everywhere. There are villages of widows and orphans. The new president stopped it. He gave rifles to the men. Now, when the guerillas or the *desconocidos* come, they die.

"But not until all the fascists die," Luis insisted, "will there be peace. We must kill them all. When the new president came, I believed all would be good. But the war continues. The rich still have their armies of *desconocidos*. The EGP hides in the mountains. Unomundo still lives..."

Luis's voice drifted away as he stared at the highway, his face lit green from the dashboard lights. Mechanically he steered through the curves, maintaining an even speed. Lyons sat in thought. He had read of the terrorism in the remote villages, but the North American newspapers always described the attacks as "Army atrocities." He had read endless diatribes against the government, but Lyons had never really read the truth.

After a minute, Luis spoke of his own sorrow.

"I managed a trucker's cooperative. Many trucks, many drivers. Garages and gasoline stations. But we would not work for Unomundo. So his killers came for me. I was not there. I escaped death. But my wife and baby did not. With machetes...."

Luis went silent. He drove by reflex, his mind trapped in a numbing nightmare. Miles later, he suddenly said:

"Now I fight. Why do you fight?"

After what Luis had told him, what could Lyons say? Had he suffered like Luis? Or like Dr. Orozco? Lyons had not lost his family to psychopathic monsters. True, years before, Mafia hoods had beaten and whipped him for a week, but within a few months he had healed. The experience had scarred him, hardened his character, but he had suffered no trauma.

As the landscape of fields and mountains drifted past, Lyons reconsidered his life. Why did he fight? Memories of his years as a police officer in Los Angeles came in a rush: the scenes of felons' mindless cruelty to their victims; the elderly broken for a snatched dollar; the bank clerks with their lives draining through wounds; the workers crippled or murdered for their paycheck; the children tortured and strangled to satisfy lust; the wide-eyed, slashed corpses of women—teenagers, mothers, grand-mothers—raped and then murdered, sometimes murdered then raped, and dumped like trash.

He thought of the parole boards that considered the families of victims annoying obstacles to the swift release of convicts. He recalled the courts that gave child-rapists five trials to perfect their defense. And the psychiatrists who excused any atrocity as a product of society's errors. And the utopians who petitioned the government to disarm society, to leave good people defenseless against the predators. And the industries glamorizing the drug gangs and criminals.

These things explained his rages, his passion for justice. But why did he fight?

Lyons had many excuses not to fight. As a taxpayer, he paid others to fight—police, teenage army recruits, air force pilots. As a robust male, no one personally threatened him. As a worker with skills and income, he could hire security guards to protect his home and office. As a man of some intelligence, he could easily rationalize noninvolvement. Why did he fight?

"Because I can. I'm strong, I'm fast, I get stupid when I'm angry, then I do brave things. I don't think about death except in the middle of the night. That's why." His explanation had come after a long pause.

"You have a wife? Children?" Luis asked.

"She divorced me. Couldn't take going to other policemen's funerals and waiting for mine. Couldn't take me twitching at night when I couldn't forget what I'd seen. Isn't easy for a woman to be married to a policeman."

"Why do you fight here?"

"Unomundo killed Federal agents in the United States. I wish my government had not waited for them to die. If we had come years ago, maybe they'd still be alive. Maybe your family would still be alive. There's a hundred places I wish I'd gone to fight when I had the chance. North America. South America. Here. Some nights I think of what I could have done and didn't and I'm ashamed."

Luis laughed. "You talk like a missionary."

"Yeah, yeah," Lyons agreed, laughing with the Guatemalan. "But they bring the Word. I bring the Wrath."

They came to a crossroads and took another highway. The hours passed. Cornfields and gardens became vertical hillsides. Winding upward through ravines, switching back every few hundred yards, the narrow road cut through a forest.

At many of the curves, their headlights revealed clusters of small crosses. Names marked the crosses. Rotting flowers indicated frequent visits by mourners. Beyond the guardrails, the wooded mountainside dropped away to darkness.

"Why the graves there?" Lyons asked.

"Not graves. Shrines. That is where they died, so their families believe that is where their spirits wander."

"EGP? The Nazis?"

"No. Buses. Cars."

The switchbacks and curves continued, the highway zigzagging ever higher. Mist swirled in the headlight beams.

Lyons awoke to see a half moon over a town, the whitewashed walls a bluish white against the night. He thought he dreamed. The image of the town surrounded by the mountains and forest seemed impossible, unreal. Then the road angled down a ridge, and they left the view behind. Lyons looked at his watch. Almost dawn.

"Where are we?"

"In the Sierra de Chuacus."

"Great. Where's that?"

"Perhaps another hour to Azatlan."

In the back seat, Señora Garcia slept. Lyons saw the headlights of the Volkswagen a few hundred yards behind them. He keyed his hand-radio.

"How are you two holding up?"

"This is the scenic route," Gadgets bantered, "no doubt about it. But the government didn't send us here to shoot picture postcards "

"The man says another hour to the town."

"Lights! Lights behind me, coming up fast!"

Luis heard the words shout from the hand-radio. As the blond American slipped his Atchisson out of the guitar case, he brought the car to a halt against the hillside. He killed the lights, then took a folded-stock Galil from the floor of the Dodge. Both men stepped into the predawn chill. They took cover behind the car.

"We've stopped," Lyons told his partners. "Make it past us. If they're trying an intercept, we'll blow them away."

"Oh, man! They're gaining on us. And if they don't get us, the next curve will."

Headlights streaked through the network of branches downslope. Bracing his Atchisson's fourteen-inch barrel on the trunk lid, Lyons flicked the fire-selector to full-auto and waited.

An air horn blared. Careening around a hairpin turn below them, tires sliding on the mist-slick asphalt, the Volkswagen van raced what looked like a truck. The second pair of headlights almost touched the van's back bumper, then the vehicle swerved into the oncoming lane to pass. The air horn sounded again.

Squinting against the glare, Lyons aimed at the

center of the pursuers' truck. He heard the click of the safety on the Galil that Luis held. But then Luis said:

"It is nothing. Only a bus."

"What? Passing on a mountain curve?"

At seventy miles an hour, the Ford thirty-eight-seat bus hurtled past. Lyons saw a teenager sitting on the dashboard next to the driver, leaning back against the windshield, reading a comic book by the beam of a flashlight. Its horn warning downhill traffic, the bus downshifted for the next curve, and took it seemingly on two wheels. They heard the engine roar up the next stretch of road above them, then the warning horn as the bus roared on its way along the up-and-down switchback road.

Lyons set his assault-shotgun's safety. "Take the bus and leave the suicide to us...."

Autofire ripped the quiet. Lyons dropped down and keyed his hand-radio.

"Wizard! Pol! Stop, someone's shooting up there."

The Volkswagen swerved off the asphalt near the Dodge. Jerking the parking brake, Blancanales jumped from the driver's door, his M-16/M-203 over-and-under in his hands. Gadgets followed an instant later, a captured Galil in one hand, a bandolier of magazines in the other.

In the graying darkness, Able Team gathered together and crouched in the roadside brush, listening. Mist glistened on pines and oaks. Drops of moisture fell through the leaves, some falling on the warriors' hands and weapons. But they heard no more shots. Lyons whispered to the others.

"I'm going for a look."

Jamming an extra magazine of seven 12-gauge shells in his jacket pocket, Lyons ran uphill along the road. The mist chilled his face as he labored against the incline. His lungs ached as he tried to gulp oxygen from the thin air. The 9,000-foot altitude defeated his sprint. He slowed to a jog, then a panting walk.

After a half-circle curve, the road continued straight. Lyons went flat on the asphalt at the end of the curve. He scanned the straight section. He saw nothing moving. Above the roadway, beyond the overarching pine branches, the sky became gray with dawn.

Lyons did not chance walking on the road. He slung his Atchisson over his back and snaked across the asphalt to the other side. Clutching at roots, his soft-soled shoes finding footholds in the rocks, he went hand-over-hand up the embankment.

The exertion made him gasp. He slowed his climbing. He disciplined his breathing, pulling down long, deep gulps of moist air, matching his breath cycles to his motions. He pulled himself through the roots and ferns and rocks very quietly, only the slight sound of falling pebbles and dirt breaking the silence.

Voices came from above. He froze, listening for the source. In the tangle of pines and oaks growing from the near-vertical mountainside, some of the voices seemed distant, others near. He inched up the slope as if crawling up a wall.

An obstacle stopped him. He made out the rusting, dismantled form of a car—doors and interior and motor gone—propped against a pine. A broken guardrail lay amidst cut branches. He could not continue to the road above without thrashing through the debris. He looked to the sides. More debris blocked him. For years, road maintainance crews had simply dumped trash and tree trimmings downhill.

He looked at the pines. Fifty to sixty to a hundred feet tall, the trees rose high above the road. Branches grew from the trunks in all directions.

Lyons climbed silently up a pine, keeping the trunk between him and the voices. In seconds, he was looking down at the road.

The mist glowed red with taillights. Soldiers in the camouflage uniform of the Army of Guatemala paced the road in front of the stopped bus. Flashlights swept the interior of the vehicle, casting silhouettes against the windows. Soldiers checked identity cards.

Laughter came from the pickup trucks and a troop carrier parked against the side of the mountain. Lyons heard English.

A flashlight revealed a blond soldier. Lyons saw an M-16 in the soldier's hands. Another soldier, this one over six feet tall, his bulk indicating a weight of two hundred pounds, carried an M-60 machine gun. A belt of ammunition went over his shoulder.

Eventually the mercenaries waved the bus on.

Now, at last, Lyons knew why the bus drivers of the *Terminal Extraurbanos* hated him and Blancanales. They had assumed the two North Americans had come to their country to serve as pro-fascist mercenaries for Unomundo. He keyed his hand-radio and whispered:

"We got problems."

Ten minutes later, the sky becoming blue, Blancanales and Luis climbed up nearby trees along the road. Lyons signaled Gadgets.

"Ready."

The Volkswagen's horn answered him. On the road, the mercenaries heard the honking. They flicked away cigarettes. Fanning out across the road, they took positions to block the approaching car.

Lyons saw the headlights of the Volkswagen far below him. The horn sounded twice to alert oncoming vehicles, then the vehicle swept around the curve. The mercenaries waited. As Gadgets neared the next hairpin turn, the horn sounded twice again.

The mercenaries waited. No car appeared.

An officer called out in an American accent. "Mitchell! Run down the road and see what's going on."

Fire from Lyons's Atchisson smashed down merc after merc, each blast sending double-ought and number-two steel shot ripping through a chest. A 40mm fragmentation round popped at the far end of the line of troop trucks, a thousand high-velocity razors shredding a line of men. Luis fired an instant later.

A blond pro-fascist dodged through the cross fire and dived for cover under a truck. Lyons hit him with a two-shot storm of steel, throwing him sideways in the air. The guy tried to crawl, but one arm flopped uselessly at his side, the humerus bone shattered. The dying merc screamed throughout the remaining seconds of the slaughter, blood frothing from his mouth and chest.

Two men sprinted out of the kill zone, spinning around to spray bursts from their M-16 rifles. Slugs ripped through the branches of the trees. Lyons swung his weapon to sight on the running men but their downhill sprint took them out of his line of fire. A burst from Luis hit one man. He fell, rolled, lost his weapon, scrambled to his feet. Blood spread from a long wound across his back, but the mercenary continued running.

An autoweapon flashed from the curve. Single shots from Gadgets's captured Galil found the merc and dropped him. More slugs tore through the chests of fleeing mercenaries. One man fell down the slope of roadside trash, another died where he crouched behind a truck.

Lyons emptied the second magazine of 12-gauge shells. Slinging his Atchisson, he scanned the road for life. Only Luis fired now, burst after burst raking the dead and dying, silencing the screamers, then killing the dead again.

"Stop firing!" Blancanales shouted.

Silence returned to the mountains.

9

In the uniforms of Unomundo's mercenaries, in captured vehicles, Able Team drove on to Azatlan. Only minutes had passed since they had annihilated the platoon of foreign pro-fascists and Guatemalan traitors manning the roadblock. After gathering an assortment of matériel—four camouflaged uniforms, walkie-talkies, an M-60, an Uzi, a few boxes of 12 gauge rounds, a bandolier of 40mm grenades—they dumped the other weapons, all the corpses and a troop truck off the steep edge of the road. Only bloodstains and cartridge casings marked the site of the slaughter.

Gadgets and Blancanales had abandoned the rented car after transferring their gear from the Volkswagen to a bullet-pocked pickup truck. Now, with a full-powered vehicle, they followed the Dodge at sixty miles an hour through the twists and hairpin curves of the highway, finally reaching the crest of the mountain in full daylight.

They looked down through drifting clouds to Azatlan. In a valley between vertical mountains, surrounded by rolling hills and a patchwork of fields, the village straddled the sun-flashing thread of a stream. The asphalt road came to an end at the central square. A dirt track continued north to the next range of mountains. Another road cut to the west and disappeared into the cliffs and forests. Other than the asphalt highway, Azatlan had no paved streets.

In the morning light, the whitewashed church and rows of houses gleamed. Smoke drifted up from kitchen fires. Azatlan seemed to be a vision of peace and simplicity from another time.

But the long lines that streaked the fields west of the village destroyed the illusion.

Blancanales scanned the fields with binoculars. "See those tire tracks? Cutting across—"

"Yeah," Lyons agreed. "They've been landing planes there."

"Don't see a building big enough to serve as a warehouse." Blancanales swept the eight-power optics over the dirt roads. "But they could be trucking the stuff into the mountains—"

"Question is," Gadgets interrupted, "why would they have an arsenal out here? Ain't exactly a central location."

Nodding, Blancanales returned his binoculars to the case. "And what for?"

Descending the winding road, they left the pine forests. Fields of withered brown corn covered the lower slopes. No one hoed the rows. No families lived in the scattered houses of packed earth and stone. A skeletal dog saw the Dodge and the pickup approaching and fled into the burned ruins of a house. The whitewashed walls of another house showed the scars of bullets. Lyons watched the devastation pass, his mind raging.

This is why he had come. To fight the monsters who murdered families.

Lyons thought of the Manhattan Marxists who had denounced the new president of Guatemala for arming the village militias.

As a result of the American refusal to supply the Guatemalan army with spare parts for their helicopters, the army could not respond quickly to terrorist attacks—Communist and *desconocido*—against remote towns and villages.

Unlike rural people in the United States, the farmers and workers in the mountain villages had no rifles or shotguns for self-defense against Communist raiders or the death squads. The cost of a good rifle or shotgun exceeded what a subsistence farmer could earn in a year.

The new president confronted the problem directly. Despite the violent opposition of conservatives in his country, the president issued the Guatemalan army's old semi-automatic Garands and M-1 carbines to the peasant militias. With the assistance of Army trainers, the people in the isolated villages formed self-defense militias. The violence against the innocent stopped.

But North American Marxists and misguided humanitarians protested. Through international organizations, they attempted to deny the Guatemalans the rights that protected the citizens of the United States, the constitutional right to defend their family and home against marauders, criminal or Communist or fascist.

Here, in this remote mountain valley, the Nazis had defeated both the army and the people of Guatemala. Lyons wished he could take the editorial writers of *The New York Times* on a drive through this devastation. What would they write when they returned to the comfort of their high-security apartments and police-patrolled streets?

At the outskirts of the village, they came to a checkpoint. Four soldiers in the camouflage of the Guatemalan army lounged in the shade of an avocado tree.

Luis stopped the car at the crossbar. A soldier reading a magazine looked up from the pages, then wandered over to the Dodge. The soldier glanced at Luis and Lyons and Señora Garcia. He leaned on the short end of the crossbar to raise the other end. Lyons saw the lurid cover of the soldier's magazine. Pornography, with the title printed in English.

Seeing the pickup approach, the soldier left the crossbar up for Gadgets and Blancanales. He returned to his magazine, not even looking up as the second vehicle passed.

Lyons keyed his hand-radio. "Those soldiers weren't Guatemalan."

Blancanales answered. "Two of them were Puerto Rican or Cuban. I don't know about the others. Quiz the Señora again."

"Definitely an international operation," Lyons added, then clicked off. He turned to the woman in the back seat. "Now you'll take us to your contact."

Her hair was matted from sleeping on the seat. Her face was puffy. She nodded. "The captain of police. I take the messages to him."

"And does he take the messages to Unomundo?" Lyons asked her.

"I don't know."

"Whenever you've come out here, have you seen mercenaries in the village?"

"Yes. No—I see them on the roads. Sometimes in Azatlan."

"There a place where they hang out? A bar? A brothel?"

"I take the messages to the captain of the police. I know nothing of these other things. I know nothing. I tell you a thousand times, but you do not hear."

"Same story," Lyons radioed Blancanales. "She takes it to the police. But if the local cops are any good, they'll know where the place is, even if Unomundo won't tell the police captain. We'll put questions to them."

Low-gearing through the village, they saw boarded-up windows, streets without people. In the central square, no vendors displayed goods or vegetables or meats in the market stalls. A face peered quickly from a window, then a shutter slammed shut.

Patterns of bullet holes dotted the whitewashed church. Sheet-metal doors bore the dents and holes of autofire. Across a dirt street from the church, an Anglo pro-fascist talked with a policeman. The Anglo wore an unfamiliar uniform, not green camouflage like the other mercenaries but gray. The policeman and the mercenary looked up at the approaching car and pickup truck. Lyons turned to Señora Garcia and warned her:

"We're walking straight in. You make a problem, you die on the spot."

As Luis parked, Lyons watched the policeman and the mercenary. An M-1 carbine leaned against the wall of the police station. The mercenary wore a Colt .45 in a black nylon holster and web belt. The two men returned to their conversation.

Lyons warned Señora Garcia one more time. "We've got your children and your husband back in the city. Walk straight in, help us get the man we want, and you can go home to your family."

Leaning over the seat, Lyons put his knife to the plastic bands looped around her ankles. He freed her ankles, then her wrists.

She threw open the door, screamed. "*Comunistas! Ayudeme!* The Communists took me prisoner! Kill them!"

A three-round burst from the Atchisson tore the policeman and the pro-fascist apart, spraying blood and shredded flesh over the white wall.

Sprinting after the woman, Lyons caught her in the doorway of the police station. He smashed the rubber-padded steel butt of the assault shotgun down on her head to stun her.

Inside, a policeman grabbed a long-barreled Remington shotgun from a wall rack and pumped the action. A blast of steel ripped his head away. Lyons scanned the room. He saw a heavy locked door with a barred window. A second door had a sign: CAPTAIN.

Kicking the police captain's door, Lyons ducked back. Three pistol shots popped inside. Plaster fell as the bullets punched into the ceiling.

"Give up or die!" Lyons yelled.

No more shots came. Lyons threw a chair into the office. No shots. He snapped a glance inside, and saw an open window.

Autofire suddenly hammered the outside wall, slugs breaking the window glass and punching into the interior of the office. Lyons took another quick

into the room to make sure the captain was not
ing against the wall. No one there.

Lyons dashed outside. The captain of police lay
ead outside the window. As Lyons arrived, Luis
fired a burst through the man's head, disintegrating
the skull.

"You dumb bastard!" Lyons screamed at him.

"He tried to escape."

Rushing back to the front entrance, Lyons looked
for Gadgets and Blancanales. He did not see their
pickup truck. He keyed his hand-radio.

BLANCANALES KICKED DOWN THE DOOR of an abandoned house. He moved to a window and smashed
out the nailed-closed shutters. Gadgets carried in the
captured M-60 machine gun.

The window looked out onto the road into town.
Blancanales keyed his hand-radio to answer Lyons.

"We're on the other side of the square. We're—"

The jeep raced toward the sound of gunfire at the
police station. Its fascist force of four leveled their
rifles to fire across the square at Lyons. Gadgets
sighted the M-60 and pulled the trigger.

Slugs slammed the jeep. The windshield shattered.
The continuous line of high-velocity 7.62 NATO
punched through the mercenaries in the front seat
and continued through the bodies of the men in the
back. Gadgets held the trigger back, the heavy weapon jackhammering in his hands, Blancanales guiding the belt of cartridges. Tracers passed through
bodies, ricocheted off steel, streaked into the distance.

The jeep hurtled out of control through the square,

the soldiers aboard dead, their chests and heads masses of torn meat. Gadgets swung the M-60 around and gave the jeep a last burst through the side. Gasoline flamed. The jeep crashed into the square's stone fountain. It burned.

Blancanales keyed his hand-radio. "Got them."

Lyons whooped into his radio. They heard his voice simultaneously from their hand-radios and from across the square. "Let's get out of here!"

Dragging the unconscious woman to the Dodge, Lyons threw her in and slammed the door. Luis ran from the alleyway. He got in and started the engine. Lyons glared at him as he accelerated backward.

"You could have taken the captain alive."

"Why should the fascists live?" Luis asked. Whipping the wheel around, he jammed the shift into drive and put the gas pedal to the floor. Tires screeched as the stench of burning rubber filled the car.

"Not the highway!" Lyons shouted. "West. Take the dirt road to the west."

The Dodge careered through the narrow streets, bouncing on its heavy-duty suspension. Luis whipped the steering wheel from side to side to swerve around potholes. Rocks gouged at the oilpan and undercarriage. Blancanales and Gadgets followed only seconds behind.

They left Azatlan at sixty miles an hour. Passing through dry, untended cornfields, the well-maintained dirt road went due west toward the forest. In minutes, they had passed over two hills and left the village far behind.

Clusters of abandoned houses, their walls scorched, their burned roofs collapsed, dotted the fields. Rutted lanes linked the houses to the road. But Lyons saw that trucks had not followed the lanes. Instead, tire tracks scarred fields hand-tended and nurtured for generations. He spoke into his radio.

"We're cutting for the tree line. Konzaki said these Nazis have helicopters. We've got to get out of sight."

"Second the motion," Gadgets answered.

"There!" Lyons pointed to a narrow dirt lane cutting between two abandoned cornfields.

Slowing, Luis eased the big Dodge between two walls made of piled volcanic stone. Metal shrieked as rocks scraped the bodywork. Lyons snapped a full magazine into his Atchisson. He thumbed more shells into the spent magazine, then replaced it in the bandolier.

Blancanales drove straight across the cornfields. Bouncing and slamming over the rows, the pickup overtook the Dodge. Luis maintained the best speed he could without destroying the car. They passed stands of banana and avocado trees. In the yards of abandoned farms, unpicked fruit broke the branches of small trees. The lane meandered from farm to farm. Every group of houses had been burned. Walls were pocked with bullet and grenade-fragment scars.

They reached the pines. The forest showed the care of generations of woodcutters. No brush or fallen branches tangled the forest. Trees grew in spaced intervals. Near each stump, the peasant foresters had planted saplings to replace the harvested tree.

With the transmission in first and the accelerator floored, the torque of the Dodge's engine pulled the heavy sedan up the grassy slopes of the forested foothills. Luis maintained an angle almost parallel to the hillside. Soon the Dodge tilted sideways at forty-five degrees. Every bump and lurch threatened to roll the car.

But the pines did not screen them from airborne observation. Lyons called his partners.

"Think the pickup can keep going uphill?"

"Not much," Blancanales answered.

"Time to walk."

Luis found the best overhead cover and parked. Blancanales stopped beside the Dodge. Able Team assembled their gear. In addition to the gear issued by Stony Man Farm, they now had the weight of captured weapons and ammunition. Gadgets carried a folding-stock Galil rifle. Lyons packed an Uzi captured at the roadblock as a backup assault weapon.

Unfolding a satellite map of the area, Blancanales showed Luis a safe route back to the highway. "Over this mountain, follow the ridgeline of the next line of hills east. Even with the woman slowing you down, you should reach the road before dark."

"She will not slow me."

They knew what Luis intended. Lyons shook his head.

"Don't you kill her—"

"Why do you protect the fascist whore?"

"Let Unomundo take her," Lyons said. "Give us a few hours head start, then let her go where the mercs can find her. They'll be searching for us, but they'll find her. People in the town saw her lead us here. Think of it as justice."

"Tell me of justice! They took machetes to my baby, then to my wife. Her feet, her legs, her hands, her arms. I will not give this whore to Unomundo. She is mine. She will suffer *my* justice.''

Lyons went to the Dodge. He jerked the woman from the car. A shove sent her staggering down the hillside. ''Run! This is the last chance you get.''

She sprawled in the grass. Blood matted her hair. Her throat was choked with sobs. Crying, she stared around her at the men she thought would kill her.

But the three men of Able Team shouldered their packs and walked into the trees. Marching through the cool wind-swayed shadows of the pines, Lyons turned.

He saw Luis open the trunk of the Dodge. The young man took out a machete and a tangle of rope. Luis moved toward Señora Garcia. The Nazi courier staggered to her feet and stumbled away. Luis pursued her down the hill. Lyons turned away and followed his partners into the mountains.

They heard screams.

''He's chopping her up,'' Lyons told Gadgets and Blancanales.

Rotorthrob drowned out the screams. Instinctively, Able Team dropped into the dusty grass. Each one of them looked up to see a Cobra gunship skim the treetops.

Blancanales squinted into the branch-broken sky as the throb diminished. ''They couldn't have spotted us!''

But as he spoke, the rotornoise changed. The Cobra was returning.

10

WHEELING AGAINST THE SKY, the Cobra gunship dropped down to treetop level. The ripsaw sound of mini-Gatlings firing six thousand rounds a minute of 7.63 NATO struck a particular fear in Gadgets and Blancanales. During the Vietnam War, they had seen the mini-Gatlings of gunships reduce People's Army of Vietnam soldiers into nauseating heaps of chopped flesh and rags. Now, in the Sierra de Chuacus of Guatemala, a Cobra came at them.

Fire flashed from the gunship's rocket pods.

But the rockets exploded three hundred yards downslope. Gasoline flames rose into the sky.

"It's Luis they spotted!" Blancanales shouted out. "Not us. They're hitting the cars."

"Time to make distance." Lyons broke into a jog.

Laboring against gravity and thin oxygen, they force-marched uphill. They followed woodcutter trails overgrown with grass. Behind them, the Cobra ripped into the mountainside again and again with its mini-Gatlings. Flames sent a black column of smoke into the clear morning sky.

The ridge crest offered a vista of the valley. They dropped their packs and found concealment. Binoculars revealed the Cobra's markings. On the gray-painted fuselage, the black letters stood out: UNO.

From the mountains to the west, gray troop trucks raced into the valley in a cloud of dust. One truck stopped to offload a platoon of gray-uniformed soldiers. Two other trucks cut across the fields, their wheels leaving deep ruts.

"The goons on the road are the blocking force," Blancanales told Lyons. "The other two squads will sweep down from the hills. We have to watch for troopships dropping ambush teams up ahead of us."

Circling the flaming truck and car, the Cobra fired two more rockets. Metallic fire enveloped the hillside.

Gadgets whistled. "They ain't messing around. White phosphorous."

"Well, sports fans," Lyons ended their minute of observation, "we're wasting time. Think Luis got away?"

Blancanales shook his head. "Ashes to ashes."

They left the ridge crest. Following overgrown sheep trails along the south face of the mountain, they left the Cobra and the burning forest miles behind. The pines grew thicker. Clouds swept over the mountain slopes. Able Team walked from brilliant midday sunlight to swirling mist to cool shadowy forest. Like flames in the half-light, the red and pink and soft purple of the orchidlike flowers called Bromeliad graced branches above the trail.

Walls of black volcanic stone stopped them. Hiking north, they returned to the ridge crest that overlooked the valley of Azatlan. They crouched in a tangle of ferns to consider their next move.

Lyons pointed to the valley below them. "If we follow that road—"

"Unomundo's mercs will spot us," Blancanales told him.

Lyons offered another idea. "If we can find a trail up those cliff faces, we might come down behind the base. It only took a few minutes for his troops to show up once they got the alarm. I figure the base is maybe five miles to the west. What's the vote? We climb?"

Gadgets nodded. "Beam me up, Scottie, I'm tired of walking."

Laughing, Able Team searched for a trail. When they found the pathway leading up the cliffs, what they saw stopped their jokes.

A macabre display faced them.

An M-16 rifle with a twisted, corroded receiver had been jammed butt-down into the rocks. A skull and arms had been wired to the foresight, the wire securing the upper arm bones together like the horizontal of a cross. The bones of the lower arms and hands dangled down. The skull and hanging arms created a crab creature with a grinning face and empty, staring eye sockets. Cloth torn from gray fatigues added a bow-tie beneath the skull. Shreds of sun-withered flesh and sinew still clung to the bones.

"Oh, man..." Gadgets shook his head. "Mucho, mucho weirdo."

"One of Unomundo's goons," Lyons decided. He stepped closer.

"DON'T!" Blancanales shouted out. The ex-Green Beret pulled Lyons back. "Stand back, just stand back."

While Gadgets and Lyons watched, Blancanales surveyed the dust and rocks. The rifle and bones stood a few steps to the side of the trail. Blancanales circled around the rocks that held the rifle's plastic stock. He nodded to himself. Pointing into the rocks, he told them:

"Don't move. Look around for any sinkholes in the trail."

"Booby traps?" Gadgets asked.

"Probably not on the trail. People with sandals have walked the path in the last day or so. But there's a land mine in front of Mr. Bones here and a grenade attached to the rifle."

"Someone around here," Gadgets said, circling a gaze at the pine forest and volcanic cliffs, "doesn't like Nazis...."

"And they're willing to do something about it," Lyons mused, playing with the philosophy, with his recent thoughts.

"Schwarz, look at this," Blancanales said. "Doesn't this look like something the Rhade would do?"

"What a flash! A freaked-out Montagnard spook show to make the 'Pavin' jump and twitch." Gadgets meant the People's Army of Viet Nam. "Most definitely indigenous ju-ju."

"Hate to break up this trip down memory lane," Lyons interrupted, "but us foreigners are standing out here in the open. Just like Mr. Bones there did, once upon a time."

"Yes, Mr. Lyons," Blancanales agreed. "That is a point. We go."

Grunting with the weight of their gear and weapons, they climbed high above the valley. A cool wind chilled the sweat that soaked their camouflage fatigues.

Sometimes clouds touched the sheer cliffs, like huge surges of white water breaking against a sea-wall.

The mist concealed them for minutes, shaded them from the searing tropical sun, then swept past as the gentle wind carried the clouds away.

Far below, through their binoculars, they saw trucks on the road. Even with the eight-power optics, Azatlan remained only a pattern of white specks. Lyons scanned the panorama of valley and hills and forest. He grinned to his partners.

"No matter what happens, this is great. I'd pay to come here."

Gadgets nodded. "Government work has its advantages."

Steel clinked on stone. In an instant, the three men disappeared into the jagged rocks. They waited, their weapons ready, off safety, their trigger fingers outside the trigger guards.

Three Indians—a young boy, a girl, and their mother—descended the trail. The woman, with a basket of fruit balanced on her head, wore a resplendent *huipile* of iridescent purple and red, the purple shoulders zigzagged with electric lines of red and pink and sky blue. She had a plastic mesh shopping bag tucked into the red and purple sash around her black skirt. Like the mother, the girl wore the same purple and red *huipile* and black skirt.

The boy wore white pants and a black hand-woven shirt. He ran along the trail, chasing lizards with a machete. Weaving through the rocks, he came face-to-face with Lyons.

Laughing at the boy's surprise, Lyons lowered his Atchisson. The boy swung the blade with both hands at Lyons's head.

Lyons rolled back. He deflected the blade with the muzzle of his autoshotgun. The boy pressed the attack, raising the blade high above his head to chop down on the camouflage-clad foreigner.

Kicking the boy in the chest, Lyons knocked him down. The little girl screamed, the mother whipped a Colt Government Model from under her *huipile*.

Blancanales voice boomed: *"Alto! Por favor! No estamos soldados de Unomundo! Amigos! Amigos de Guatemala, venimos aquí con ayuda para ustedes!"*

Cajoling the woman in Spanish, Blancanales finally persuaded her to lower the Colt. A four-way interrogation developed as he questioned the three Indians, the Indians questioned Blancanales, and the Indians questioned one another in their language.

Lyons and Gadgets watched as their partner displayed a bullet hole in his captured uniform. Blancanales pointed out the tiny entry hole, the rinsed-out bloodstain, then the tear where the exiting slug and flesh had exploded outward. He stepped over to the other two North Americans in camouflage uniforms, and pointed out the holes and bloodstains to the Indians. He explained to his partners:

"These people know all about Unomundo. He's been using the local men for forced labor. Sometimes for target practice. The boy thought you were one of the mercenaries because of your blond hair. He thought you were alone, so he tried to kill you. Nothing personal.''

"Will they help us?" Lyons asked.

"Most definitely," Blancanales smiled. "All these bullet holes make us guests of honor."

"Ask them who did Mr. Bones," Gadgets suggested.

Blancanales asked the woman. She made a nasal-guttural Indian sound in her throat and shook her head. He translated: "I don't think she knows."

The Indians led them up the path. Gadgets struck up a friendship with the boy when he demonstrated his silent Beretta on a lizard. The boy had started after the creature with his machete. Gadgets stopped him. Slipping out the autopistol, Gadgets gripped the weapon with both hands and shot off the lizard's head. The only sound was the rush of the subsonic bullet through the air, and the noise of the bullet hitting the rocks and whining away.

The boy laughed. He held out his hand for the pistol. Gadgets shook his head as he returned it to his shoulder holster. The boy looked downcast. Gadgets held up one finger, the boy nodded.

Checking the fire-selector, Gadgets helped the boy grip the pistol. He fired a shot at the rocks. They heard only the ricochet. Gadgets took the pistol back as the boy laughed and jumped with joy.

He and the boy continued ahead of the others.

Together they walked point. The trails cut along the vertical face of the cliff, angling always upward. Once, Gadgets peered over the edge. He looked down on the others' heads a hundred feet below him. If he kicked a rock off the edge, they would be in danger.

Despite the climb, the miles passed quickly. The cool mountain air, the beauty of the valley and mountain, made the march a pleasure for the ex-Green Beret.

Gadgets and the boy reached the top before the others. On the mountain crest, the ever-present moisture of the drifting clouds created a paradise of green, knee-high grass, wild flowers, and dense pine forest. Gadgets went to the cliff edge and keyed his hand-radio.

"Shangri-la calling. All is cool."

"On our way."

The boy whistled. Following the sound, Gadgets walked along the cliff. The boy waved to him from the incomplete frame of a house. Built only a few steps back from a sheer thousand-foot drop, the front window—framed but with no glass—had a hundred-mile view.

Sitting down on the weathered flooring and piles of hand-sawn planks, Gadgets saw three mountain ranges. Smoke from the burning forest where Luis had died grayed the valley of Azatlan. But the next valley had clear air. He saw green patchworks, the thin line of a highway. Perhaps thirty miles away, smoke rose from a village, only the smoke visible, the houses and streets and churches lost in the hills and forest.

The horror of Unomundo seemed so far away, beyond possibility. Yet Gadgets knew what he saw was the illusion, and that the terror of Unomundo was the reality. He looked at the unfinished house. Apparently, Unomundo had driven them out.

You'll get yours, Mr. Nazi, Gadgets muttered to

himself. *I'm gonna sic the Ironman on you. You'll never forget him. But then again, maybe you'll get lucky and just drop dead of fright.*

Rotorthrob exploded behind him. Gadgets went flat as a gray shape flashed over him. He radioed to the others.

"Hit it! Helicopter! Looks like a Huey."

He waited for the helicopter to drop below him before moving. Holding his hand-radio, Gadgets crawled to the edge of the cliff.

A soldier squatted at the door of the gray-painted Huey troopship. Gadgets saw the mercenary searching the cliffs and trails with binoculars. The soldier pointed.

Hundreds of feet below him, Gadgets saw the bright purple and red of the Indian woman. Caught in an open stretch of the trail, Lyons and Blancanales and the two Indians ran for cover. But too late.

The helicopter veered for the cliffs. The soldier in the door pointed the swivel-mounted M-60. The muzzle flashed. Gadgets heard the hammering of the shots an instant later. Far below, dust puffed on the trail. But his partners and the Indians had gained cover. His hand-radio buzzed.

"They caught us in the open," Lyons reported. "Now it's a shoot-out. If we don't make it, it's up to you to complete the mission."

Over the radio, Gadgets heard the thumping and ricocheting of heavy-caliber slugs. Then the hammering of the M-60 drifted toward him.

"Forget that kind of talk!" Gadgets told him. "We'll get them!"

"With rifles?" Lyons asked him. "Might as well

throw rocks. But we'll shoot at them until the Cobra shows up. Then we're dead. Over and *adios*."

A few hundred feet below, the door gunner raked the cliffside trail with burst after burst. Gadgets knew what Lyons had said was the truth.

When the Cobra came, his partners died.

11

THE HUEY SEEMED TO FLOAT BELOW HIM. Gadgets
Schwarz considered his options. With his Galil, he
might hit the door gunner. But from this angle, he
could not expect the lightweight 5.56mm slugs to
punch through the pilots' windshield. Even if he
waited for a straight-on shot, the windshield would
deflect the 5.56mm slugs at wild angles. He would
have to kill the pilot and copilot simultaneously and
instantly to drop the Huey. And if he did not make
an instant kill, they would come to kill him. Like
Lyons said, he might as well throw rocks.

Rocks?

As Gadgets watched, the helicopter made another
pass at the trail, the door gunner spraying Lyons
and Blancanales with a long burst. A soldier threw
a grenade. The explosion puffed dust on the cliff
face.

Gadgets grabbed a fist-sized rock and threw it. He
watched the angle of fall.

He ran back from the edge. Frantically searching
through the clutter of materials stacked around the
unfinished house, he found rolls of barbed wire and
chicken wire. Rough-sawn planks leaned against the
house.

He tore off the weather-rotted cardboard on the

end of a roll of barbed wire. He dragged the roll of wire to the cliff.

He watched the helicopter. The Huey had completed a circle and was veering in for another attack. The M-60 flashed fire.

Strong with panic, Gadgets jerked up the barbed wire from the ground. He held it above his head, then threw it.

The heavy roll of wire hit a rock and bounced far out from the cliff.

Gadgets watched. The wire fell in erratic gyrations.

It did not miss. The unraveling wire hit the circle of the Huey's rotorblades. It whirled in a tangle above the fuselage for an instant, then the blades started to buckle and twist as the wire was sucked into their spin.

A rotor flew into space. The three remaining blades locked. The Huey fell straight down. The fuselage disintegrated on the rocks, then flame rose in a sheet.

"Whoo-eee! The Wizard does it!" Lyons laughed through his hand-radio. "What a trick. Brought us back from the dead."

"I don't believe it myself."

"Watch for the Cobra," Lyons told him. "We're on our way up, double time. Maybe you'll get a chance to drop another surprise."

Beside him, the Indian boy stared down at the burning helicopter. The boy looked from the helicopter to the chicken wire and planks stacked around the house, looked down to the wreckage again. Gadgets laughed.

"When you eliminate the impossible. . ." he said.

The Cobra came three minutes later.

LYONS AND BLANCANALES directed the woman and child to take cover. The Indians crouched behind a rock, the little girl crying, the mother sobbing and shrieking, her hands over her ears as the Cobra approached.

Lyons jerked his folded black nylon windbreaker from his backpack. He crawled to the woman and the girl. Opening the jacket, he spread it over the woman's shoulders to cover the beautiful purple-and-red weaving she wore. He touched the black rocks around them, touched the black jacket, pointed to the sky.

The crying woman nodded. She held her daughter in her arms and enfolded her brilliant colors.

Blancanales radioed Gadgets. "What's the Cobra doing?"

"Skirting the cliffs. Staying back. It's—get ready."

"Ironman!" Blancanales called out.

"I know...."

Lyons shielded the woman and child with his body as the Cobra roared past. A section of the trail erupted in a string of explosions as the gunship strafed it with 40mm grenades. Rocks and bits of steel wire—spent shrapnel—showered them.

The Indian woman screamed. Lyons held her against the rock, protecting and restraining her. If she panicked....

Mini-Gatlings tore another section of trail. A one-second burst saturated a shadow with high-velocity slugs. Tracers made an orange line between the Cobra and the cliff face. Then the gunship veered away.

Their hand-radios buzzed. "It's trying to freak you," Gadgets's voice said .

"It has succeeded," Lyons answered.

"Lay cool, bro'. That ain't all it wants to do."

They heard the gunship's autogrenades rip the foothills below them, as black smoke from the burning Huey wreck drifted up the cliff face. Gadgets buzzed them again.

"Think it just killed Mr. Bones."

Easing his head from behind the rocks, Lyons looked down to see the Cobra veer away. Streaking over the valley, it disappeared behind clouds. The walls of clouds approached the cliff.

"Where'd it go?" Blancanales asked Gadgets.

"Off toward the town. You got cloud cover coming. That'll be your chance to run for it."

"Then that's the plan," Lyons agreed.

Waiting a few minutes, they did not hear the rotor-throb return. When the wall of mist enveloped the black volcanic cliff face, hiding them from airborne observation, they rushed to the top of the mountain.

Gadgets and the boy met them. Leading them under the cover of the pines, the boy stopped in a small meadow speckled with yellow wild flowers. Lyons motioned to Blancanales.

"Tell him to keep moving. They know we're here somewhere. We got to get gone."

A voice shouted from the forest. "No move! Drop weapons! Move quick, you die!"

The woman and the girl hurried away from the three North Americans. Able Team stood alone in the kill zone.

12

MIST SWIRLED THROUGH THE SHADOWED PINES. The boy ran through the flowers. He called out again and again in his Indian language. He shielded the North Americans with his body as he shouted to the ambushers.

A voice answered. "Congratulations. Xagil tells me you're okay. For that, you stay alive. But put down the rifles, please."

"Who are you?" Lyons shouted. He did not lay down his Atchisson.

"I am coming out. If you shoot, my friends kill you all."

Blancanales flipped up the safety of his M-16/ M-203. He slung the weapon over his shoulder. He looked to his partners.

"Wizard, Ironman. Be polite. Lock up."

Lyons and Gadgets set their safeties also. But Lyons held the assault shotgun ready.

A man walked from the mist. Six foot, barrel chested, he wore gray fatigues. Old bloodstains splotched the Nazi uniform like camouflage patterns. He held a Heckler & Kock G-3 rifle fitted with a three-power scope. He had a tiny 9mm Ingram machine-pistol in a hand-made leather belt holster. On his back, they saw a steel crossbow.

Though he appeared to be Indian, with dark hair and a face as dark as mahogany, a faded tattoo on his left forearm identified his nationality and told of his past:

USMC
DEATH BEFORE DISHONOR

Blancanales stepped forward and extended his hand: "Pleased to meet you, sir. I'm Rosario."

"I am Nate." The ex-Marine spoke oddly, the inflections and rhythm of his English somehow different.

"How long since you spoke English?" Blancanales asked.

"A long time. I speak Quiche now. Sometimes Castilian—Spanish."

Lyons stared, his mouth gaping open. Gadgets slung his Galil. Hooking his thumbs in the straps of his backpack, he walked in a circle around Nate. He saw the carved wood and hand-hammered steel of crossbow and a quiver of short arrows. A knitted bag displaying the stylized figure of a prancing horse held magazines for the G-3 and Ingram.

Nate glanced at the stranger eyeing him. Gadgets laughed.

"This guy is indigenized!"

"Who are you?" Lyons finally asked.

"I told you. Nate."

"I mean, who are you with?"

"We don't have time to talk," he answered, his words coming awkwardly. He pointed into the pines. "A world of shit comes. If you want to live, we move. Follow Xagil. I follow."

Nate and the woman spoke quickly in Quiche. The

boy, Xagil, led Able Team through the pines. As they walked down into a ravine, the forest became dark with lush growth. Pushing aside a curtain of vines, Xagil followed a trail that tunneled through tangled vines and brush and bromeliad. Nate, the woman and the little girl walked soundlessly behind them.

After hundreds of yards without sight of the sun, they came to a crevice dropping into the interior of the mountain. A trail down a narrow ledge led to the fissure in the black stone.

Some distance along the ledge, they entered a cave. Xagil disconnected the monofilament triplines of booby traps. After Able Team and the Indians passed, Nate reconnected the monofilament lines.

Blancanales waved a flashlight over the interior of a cavern. Bats squeaked and fluttered in the shadows. The bats' eyes refracted the light like a thousand red stars.

"Where are your friends?" Lyons asked the ex-Marine.

Nate ignored the question. He went to one of the many shadows on the cavern wall and disappeared into the voids.

"Come!"

The flashlight that Blancanales held threw a weak glow on glistening black stone. The passage had once been a bubble in the molten magma of the flowing mountain. Now, the line of North Americans and Indians filed through it. Nate walked through the total darkness by memory. Able Team followed Blancanales's flashlight.

Wind rushed into their faces. Blinking against the

daylight, Able Team stepped into a cave mouth that overlooked a forested valley and mountains.

Lyons went to the edge and looked down. Hundreds of feet below, clouds drifted against the vertical wall of volcanic rock. He could see nothing above them but more rock.

Another Indian woman, actually a teenager with fine-boned, austere features, greeted Nate in Quiche. She went silent when she saw Able Team and their camouflage uniforms. Reflexively, her hand went for a pistol hidden under her *huipile*. Nate spoke to her in the Indian language as he stripped off his weapons and ammunition. He made introductions.

"My wife Marylena. Her sister Maria. Her son Xagil. And my son—"

He took a bundle from his wife's back. A baby stirred inside.

"—Tecun." He pointed to Blancanales. "Rosario. I don't know your names...."

"I'm the Wizard," Gadgets told them. He looked to Lyons. "And he's the Ironman."

Nate nodded. He spoke quickly to his wife. She went to an adjoining chamber. "We eat while we talk."

They sat at a hand-sawn and -crafted table on chairs of rough pine. Marylena returned with fruit and steaming patties of corn dough.

Gadgets held up one of the corn patties. "What are these?"

"Tamalitas. Now, you three men with false names, we will discuss why you are here."

"Unomundo's gang killed four Federal agents in

Texas," Lyons briefed Nate. "We've come to kill him."

Nate laughed. He called out to the women in Quiche, translated what the North American had said. The women laughed. He returned his attention to Able Team.

"Three men against a thousand?"

Lyons choked on a mouthful of mango. "A *thousand*?"

"He's got an army up here?" Gadgets asked.

Nate did not answer. "You have money?"

Blancanales sliced an avocado with his double-edged Gerber knife. "You'll sell us information?"

The ex-Marine's lip rose in a sneer. "*La Cia*. C-I-A. Always the same."

"Not us, man." Gadgets denied the charge. "We don't associate with those Harvard spooks."

"I know," Nate nodded. "You are Boy Scouts. Collecting butterflies. Ha, ha, ha. Now, we talk truth. I have lived here many years. It was good here. A few bandits. I killed them. A few EGP. I killed them. The army were my friends. They did not ask for my passport. Very peaceful. Then Unomundo came. For six months, it has been very bad. We cannot plant corn. They shoot our sheep and cows. Shoot many families—"

"What about the army and the police?" Lyons interrupted.

"Unomundo paid gold. Those who did not take the gold died. Men go to tell the government, but never return. Everyone is afraid. They move away."

"Why not you?" Blancanales asked.

Nate ignored the question. "Sometimes we fight

Unomundo. Then his soldiers kill everyone they find. Women, families, children, no difference. We need friends, but we need money, too. You are *Cia*. You have money. First, you pay for my barbed wire.''

"That was your place on the cliff? What a view!" Gadgets exclaimed through a mouthful of tamalita.

Rotorthrob echoed in the cave. The men of Able Team jerked around, starting from their pine chairs. In the distance, they heard explosions, then the ripsaw of mini-Gatlings. Nate laughed.

"They chop down trees with their fire superiority. Get a body count on shadows. But it is good that Xagil found you. Otherwise the *fascistas* would have found you. And God have mercy if they take you alive.''

Lyons ended the conversation. "Where is Unomundo?"

"Perhaps at his base. Maybe no."

"Where is the base?" Lyons pressed.

"Want to go there? I give you the guided tour. One thousand dollars each. Plus free prisoner for questions.''

Blancanales laughed as he opened his pack. "It's a deal.''

"In advance. Money stays with Marylena in case I do not return.''

They counted out hundred-dollar bills.

DESCENDING THROUGH A MAZE of volcanic formations and caverns, Nate led them deep into the mountain. Water trickled in the darkness beyond their flashlights. When they kicked rocks from the path, the rocks fell for seconds before hitting stone. Sometimes, the rocks fell into the void and no sound came. Nate led them through the twisting passages. From time to time, he stopped to disarm booby traps.

They came to a chamber he used as a storeroom. As their flashlights swept across neat stacks of Unomundo matériel—uniforms, tools, boots, rations, radios—Nate diffused devices scattered throughout the equipment. He selected uniforms for Able Team.

"At the base, they wear a gray uniform," he explained. "Those green ones, they only wear those to look like the army."

All the uniforms showed bloodstains. Blancanales saw a pile of wallets and other personal effects. He glanced through a wallet.

An identity card printed in German carried a photo of a young blond man. Another wallet held the card of a dead man from New Jersey. Another identified a soldier from El Salvador. Blancanales passed the wallets to Lyons and Gadgets.

"All foreigners."

"Most of his soldiers are not Guatemalan," Nate told them. "But some are."

Lyons changed into a uniform with a bullet hole in the left chest pocket. "How many of his mercs have you put down?"

"Count the uniforms. Plus many I could not strip."

"You do Mr. Bones?" Gadgets asked him.

"What?"

"The skull on the rifle."

"Yes. He was a Frenchman who raped and tortured. I made a joke of him."

"And what was their response?" Lyons buckled

on his web belt and bandoliers, then bounced on his toes to test for metal tapping against metal.

"They patrol. They try to ambush. But they are not good soldiers. They do not fight, they murder."

"And what about the weapons?" Lyons pointed to the stacked uniforms, then the three that Able Team wore. "Fourteen sets of fatigues and gear, but no rifles, no pistols. No ammunition—"

Nate stopped the questioning. "Time to go, tourists."

A few minutes later they emerged from one of the thousands of crevices and caves that pitted the mountain. Rocky hillsides sloped down to a narrow valley. Unomundo's road slashed through pine and deciduous forest. The few cleared fields had been burned.

Beyond, perhaps two miles from where they stood, the black wall of another mountain rose into the clouds. Nate pointed out the path they would take.

"There is the road to Azatlan. It goes around that mountain. Unomundo's base is on the north side. We will cross the valley and go into the mountain. The caves will take us to Unomundo."

Carrying only the weight of their weapons, the four men moved quickly. Able Team labored to maintain a steady jog despite the thin air. Nate allowed them to rest every few minutes while he ranged ahead in the forest. They crossed the dirt road without sighting mercenaries.

Distant rotorthrob drifted to them from time to time. They stayed under the cover of the trees.

Once, as they approached a clearing, their eyes searching the sky, they heard metal clanking in the rhythm of steps. Nate turned to signal Able Team.

but they had already disappeared into the grass and brush.

A line of fifty gray-clad mercenaries passed.

Minutes after the voices and footsteps had faded away, Nate saw Able Team rise silently from cover. With hand signals, he directed them to double-time. A five-minute run took them to the mountain.

Once they had entered the darkness of the subterranean passages, Nate finally spoke.

"You have been in the jungle before. Where?"

Blancanales numbered the wars and countries on his fingers. "Vietnam, Laos, Cambodia—"

"Bolivia, Brazil—" Gadgets added.

"Los Angeles," Lyons added.

Nate smiled at Lyons's joke. "I wish I had ten friends like you. We could have killed all the mercenaries."

"Doesn't say much for the quality of Unomundo's men."

Leading Able Team through the darkness of the caves, the ex-Marine answered with a sneer. "They are the best money can buy."

"What about you?" Lyons asked him. "Why aren't you working for Unomundo? Won't he pay your price?"

Lyons's question offended even the tolerant Gadgets Schwarz. "What an idiot thing to ask," he said. "Leave it to a cop to ask a question like that. Why don't *you* sign up with that Nazi warlord, Lyons?"

Nate spat out an answer. "Unomundo has a bounty on me. Ten thousand quetzales. That is ten thousand dollars, United States. And this is for me. A man with no country. But you, you are special.

Tres huevos de la Cia. I think he will pay a hundred thousand dollars for you. What do you think? Should I take top price? I take quick hundred thousand Q. I will never again need to cut wood or plant corn or shear sheep. My wife will not live in a cave, my son will have school—''

Blancanales interrupted with soothing words. ''Our friend asked the wrong question. It's just that we can't understand your one-man war against these invaders.''

Despite the questions and the argument, Nate never broke pace. He led them relentlessly upward through the cold darkness of the caves. ''What is there to understand? I live in this beautiful place, these mountains, in the forest. If a thousand murderers and rapists with machine guns came to your home, you would fight, yes?''

''I'm sorry,'' Lyons apologized. ''Sometimes I don't understand the obvious. I only wondered why you hadn't just left like all the other people.''

''Someone must fight.'' Nate ended the talk by striding far ahead. From time to time, he flashed his light back to guide them.

Gadgets hissed to Lyons: ''Be cool, will you? He's got real sensitive feelings. Besides, I think he's got a grudge against the CIA.''

''I cannot figure him. He's an American, but he's been up here for years. Maybe *he's* CIA. Maybe he's an agent who went crazy and disappeared.''

''I don't care who he is,'' Gadgets snapped back. ''He's our ticket to a quick hit. Don't piss him off.''

''Until I know what his game is, we aren't secure. We don't know who he's working for.''

"Dig it, dude, I too am a paranoid, but there is a limit." Gadgets jogged away from Lyons, leaving him to walk alone.

A few minutes later, they saw daylight.

"Wait here," Nate told them. "I check for men watching the cave, then I come back. It has happened before." He left the cave for the open air.

Lyons unholstered his silent autoColt. "I'm following him. He could be putting an ambush together."

Gadgets stared at Lyons for a moment, then turned to Blancanales. "Think we could kick his brain straight?"

Blancanales shook his head, no. "He was a policeman too many years. Go, Lyons. Go out there. Satisfy your suspicions."

Pistol in hand, Lyons slipped from the narrow cave mouth. Blinking against the afternoon glare, he pushed a wall of pine branches.

Rotorthrob shattered the quiet. Squinting against the light, Lyons looked up.

A gunship swooped down on him.

13

As the Cobra descended on him, as he sucked down the last desperate gasp of his life, Lyons pointed the silenced Colt at the gunship's armored underbelly. He knew the slugs would not even scratch the armor, but he would not die without—

A hand knocked the weapon aside, the burst of .45-caliber hollowpoints flying harmlessly into the distance. Nate pushed the autoweapon into the dust and rocks. With the weight of his body, he held Lyons motionless as the Cobra dropped past them. He shouted through the rotor roar, a storm of dust and leaves flying around them:

"It is nothing! They do not see us!"

Waiting until the noise and rotorstorm faded, they crawled through a tangle of brush and pine branches. The mountainside dropped away. Looking over the cliff, they saw trucks.

Hundreds of feet below them, gray-uniformed soldiers loaded heavy military trucks. The Cobra floated down. But the soldiers did not clear the area. As the gunship's skids seemed to touch the trucks, it veered sideways into the cliff face.

"What the—" Lyons started.

"There is a cave under here. A big cave. Many helicopters and trucks in there. Many buildings."

"And nothing's visible from the air." Lyons's mind raced ahead. "Munitions?"

Nate understood. He shook his head. "Separate cave. Very secure. Bring your friends out. They must see."

When Blancanales and Gadgets joined them on the ledge, Nate continued the briefing. "There is no way in through the mountain. Walls of concrete block the caves."

Blancanales nodded. "Have you been in there?"

"At first, before they had so many mercenaries. Not since."

"We could walk straight in," Lyons suggested. "Pass as mercenaries."

"There are many guards. Identity cards. Very difficult to... fake it."

"Time for air strikes," Gadgets suggested. Lyons and Blancanales knew he meant Jack Grimaldi, the Stony Man ace pilot.

Staring down at the mercenaries and assembled trucks, Nate shook his head. "In Laos, in the Co Roc mountains, there was a cave like this. The NVA put one hundred fifty-two mikemike guns inside, hit Khe Sanh every day for months. We tried B-52s, fighter bombers, Laotian mercenaries. *Nada*, only noise and dead men. Then us. Twenty-four Marines in, one Marine out. Me. The guns still hit Khe Sanh."

He looked to the three men of Able Team. "I tell you this, Secret Agents. If you want to hit this place, I will help you. Nothing you can think of will do it. But I can. It costs you one hundred thousand dollars. What do you say?"

"Maybe," Lyons answered.

"Yes or no?"

"The money's no problem," Blancanales told Lyons.

"That's not it. We don't know the options. Let's go get our prisoners. Put some questions to them before we talk plans."

"There is a lookout on the top." Nate glanced toward the peak. "We go there."

Sheep trails crisscrossed the near-vertical slopes. Guiding them through the pines and ferns, Nate paused often to peer at the soft grasses.

Then he found a rectangle of discolored moss. He motioned Able Team back. He took a bit of wire and string from his knitted bag.

He hooked the moss and stretched out the string. Twenty feet away, he went flat. He pulled the string. Nothing happened.

Leaving cover, they saw that a square of moss had flipped over to expose a small land mine. Blancanales recognized it instantly.

"Bouncing Bettie."

"They have many. They have killed many sheep."

Taking only a few more seconds, Nate found the safety pin and slipped it through the housing. He checked the underside for secondary detonators, then pulled the mine from the hole. He concealed it a hundred yards farther along the trail, where he could retrieve it later.

Continuing to the top, they heard shots. Nate directed them to an animal trail running under the bushes and small trees. They covered the last two hundred yards on their bellies. The shooting—single shots, sometimes an auto-burst—continued.

The observation post overlooked the valley. Plastic bags filled with dirt, stacked waist high, formed a rectangle. A camouflage-patterned canopy protected a squad of mercenaries from the sun.

The mercenaries sprawled in the shade, drinking beer and playing cards. One man scanned the late afternoon panorama of the valley, the road, and the far mountain with a telescope on a tripod. Another man with an M-16 sniped at birds soaring in the thermal updrafts.

Somewhere else on the mountaintop, another rifle—a large-caliber weapon—boomed. The distant rifleman fired single shots, sometimes three quick semi-auto shots.

"These guys," Lyons whispered to the others, "are definitely jack-offs."

Blancanales and Gadgets nodded. Nate pointed toward the sound of the other rifle. Leaving his partners to watch the squad at the observation post, Lyons followed Nate along the ridge line. They crawled, then walked silently through the lengthening shadows.

They found two mercenaries in aluminum lawn chairs. A stack of sandbags supported the shooter's exotic Walther sniper-rifle as he squeezed off shots at a target over four hundred yards away. A spotter with a telescope sat beside him, calling his hits.

Lyons put his binoculars on the target. He saw a black-and-white life-size photograph of the president of Guatemala. As he watched, the rifle boomed three times. Three holes appeared in the photograph, all in the center of the president's chest. Lyons passed the binoculars to Nate.

The spotter spoke into a walkie-talkie. Down-range, a blond soldier left cover to change targets. He stapled another life-size photo of the President to a splintered sheet of plywood.

"This fellow is a serious shooter," Lyons told Nate. "He's bound to have some interesting information. Like why he's using that particular target."

"And the others at the lookout?"

"We'll take these two, and we'll get out without those lizards even knowing we were here."

Nate grinned. "We go, spook man."

Lyons dusted off his gray uniform. He slung his Atchisson behind him. The silenced .45 went into his belt at the small of his back. He left his Python in his shoulder holster. He left cover.

He made no effort at silence as he walked up behind them. As the rifle boomed three times, the spotter turned.

"Now what?"

"Special interrogation session," Lyons told him, smashing him in the side of the head with his heavy-barreled Python. The other man grabbed at a flap-holstered Colt. The Python came down on his skull.

Nate rushed to the stunned men. In seconds, they tied the hands of both men behind them, then linked their prisoners together with ropes around their necks. Nate ripped off one man's shirt, tore it in strips, used it for blindfolds and gags.

"And the man there?" Nate pointed to the soldier changing the target.

Glancing to the western horizon, Lyons guessed they had an hour until dusk. "We got two prisoners."

"Can't leave him. He has a radio. He will—"

Lyons took the rifleman's chair. He examined the Walther 2000 semi-automatic rifle. The bulky, ultra-modern weapon utilized the "bullpup" configuration; the designers had placed the receiver group and the magazine in the buttstock, behind the grip and trigger housing. Looking at a box of cartridges, he saw that the rifle fired not 5.56mm or 7.62 NATO slugs, but Winchester .300 Magnum. He found the safety and magazine release, then dropped out the box magazine to check the cartridges. He slapped back the magazine.

Taking the walkie-talkie, he pressed the transmit, said only: "Ready?"

"Yes, sir."

He put the rifle to his shoulder. As the spotter moved away from the new photo of the president of Guatemala, Lyons put the reticle of the Leatherwood 3x-9x ART scope on the center of the man's back.

Three slugs bounced the soldier off a tree. He died before he fell.

"That'll teach him to hang around in the line of fire."

A few seconds later, after gathering up all the ammunition and packing the Walther rifle into its fiberglass and foam case, Lyons and Nate dragged their prisoners off. Nate slung his crossbow. They cut away from the lookout and followed a trail through the deep shadows of pines and chest-high ferns. Lyons walked point with his Atchisson. He buzzed Blancanales and Gadgets and whispered into his hand-radio.

"Pol, Wizard. Pull out. We got our prisoners."

Shouts came from the lookout post. Automatic fire ripped through the pines. They jerked the tied and blindfolded mercenaries to cover. Lyons spoke again into the hand-radio.

"What's going on?"

No answer. Pulling the groggy, gagged prisoners along by the rope, Nate crouchwalked to Lyons.

"To the trail!"

"Moving."

Forcing the prisoners to run blind, the four men thrashed through the ferns. As the prisoners fell, Nate dragged them to their feet and kicked them on. Lyons dropped to one knee and scanned the tree lines fifty yards away.

Nothing moved in the half-darkness of the pines. The autofire died to sputters, then single shots.

Using the prisoners as a shield, Nate ran into the open ground. Jerking at the rope linking their necks, beating them with his G-3, Nate staggered across the rocks while Lyons watched the tree line over the sights of his Atchisson.

Two mercenaries ran from the tree line. They looked behind them as they stumbled into the open. His back to the clearing, one mercenary fired a quick burst into the pines. He did not turn until Lyons killed the first man.

Whirling, the second mercenary emptied his M-16's magazine in one sweeping burst. His rifle's action locked back as high-velocity steel from Lyons's Atchisson punched a pattern of wounds through his body.

Nate and the prisoners had dropped to the ground. One man had managed to get a hand free of the bindings. Lyons saw the prisoner beat at Nate.

Autofire came from the tree line, the high-velocity slugs shrieking across the clearing. The half-free prisoner jerked the other to his feet. They stumbled for the trees.

His gray uniform bright with blood, Nate tried to rise to his feet. Aimed fire puffed dust around him. Falling on his face, Nate lost his G-3. He tried to roll to cover, screaming as he rolled onto the crossbow.

Lyons sprayed the tree line with steel, changed magazines as he sprinted to Nate. High-velocity slugs zipped past him. A slug slammed into the fiberglass rifle case slung across his back. His shoulder hit the rocks. He rolled, ran again.

More bullets tore past him. He dived into the grass. Ricocheting bullets hummed away as he searched for Nate's wound, pulling aside the tangle of shattered crossbow and straps and torn uniform.

He saw a long, curving slash in Nate's back. "You're okay, you're all right. It's not a bullet, you're just bleeding. Just a cut—" He grabbed the G-3 and pushed it into Nate's hands.

Nate grunted and tried to rise. Bullets threw dust and stones. Lyons saw a gray uniform in the tree line. He sighted his Atchisson. He fired a single shot, but too late. The form dodged back.

Taking Nate by the collar, Lyons jerked him from the ground with his left hand while his right hand pointed 12-gauge blasts at the muzzle flashing in the trees.

"Take cover, spook!" Nate gasped. "I can walk—"

"Then move it!"

Nate swore in Quiche as pain twisted his face. He staggered and fell. Lyons jerked him to his feet.

"Big bad Marine," he said. "Bet you're calling for your momma. Can't even walk."

Slugs tore past. Lyons saw a long, low fold in the grass and rocks. Still holding Nate's collar, Lyons threw himself forward, almost wrenching his arm from the socket as he jerked Nate into the shallow gully. The two men rolled in the dust. Disentangling himself from Nate and the G-3 and the fiberglass Walther case, Lyons looked for targets in the tree line.

A long burst of autofire ended the firefight. Blancanales called out.

"It's all over here."

Lyons sprinted into the trees. He saw the sniper and spotter still running. Coughing dust, his shoulder aching, he pursued them. Still linked by the rope around their necks, one man's hands still tied behind his back, they stumbled through the undergrowth. He caught them in thirty seconds. He dragged them back to the others.

Blancanales and Gadgets tended to Nate's wound. Gadgets looked up at the returning captives.

"Great. Two of them." He pointed toward the lookout position. "Nothing up there's alive. It got dangerous."

"What happened?" Lyons asked him. "When I buzzed you—"

"Everything cut loose." Blancanales ripped open Nate's blood-soaked shirt. "Another platoon came up the trail. They joined up with the observation detail. I'm about ten yards away, hoping I'm invisible under a bush. One of them comes over and makes like a dog just as you buzz me. He heard the radio.''

"No wounded?"

Gadgets shook his head. "All the wounded are dead. Then I gave their telescopes and binocs the gravity test. Over the cliff. The radio set, too. I kept some walkie-talkies for electronic countermeasures, maybe.''

"How bad am I hit?" Nate asked.

"The bullet killed your crossbow.'' Blancanales held up the bullet-splintered stock. "But the bullet didn't get you. It's this—"

Blancanales touched a four-inch shaft of wood protruding from Nate's back. "It's a splinter from your crossbow, jammed in under your shoulder blade, maybe into your ribs. You want some morphine before I jerk it out?''

Lyons stopped Blancanales as he slipped out a syrette of painkiller. "We don't have time. Besides, we can't have him stumbling around stoned.''

As he spoke, Lyons put his knee on Nate's back. He grabbed the splinter. As he pulled, Nate screamed, convulsed with pain:

"Goddaaaaaaaaaaamn you! You torturing bastard!"

Lyons laughed. He gazed at the bloody blade of hardwood. "I don't know what you're screaming about, didn't hurt me at all.''

"Here, take some antibiotics.'' Blancanales passed Nate a palmful of pills.

"Forget the post-operative care,'' Lyons snapped. "We got to move.''

Despite his injuries, Nate walked point down the mountain pathways. Only he knew the trail. He pointed his tiny 9mm Ingram ahead of him, his right arm bound against his body with strips torn from a dead merc's uniform. Lyons stayed close behind with his Atchisson.

"Thanks, spook man," Nate told him. "For helping me."

"Then stop calling me 'spook man.' We're not with the Agency."

"I know. No *Cia* would have helped me. But I call you anything I want. Don't like it, go home."

"Anything you say, Geronimo."

Nate laughed. "You and me, we could be friends."

The captured sniper and spotter slowed them as they raced against dusk to the crack in the stone above the cave-fortress of Unomundo. Finally, Nate found the entrance by moonlight.

FAR INTO THE MOUNTAIN, they questioned the prisoners. Lyons cut their gags.

"Why the pictures of the president?" he asked.

The rifleman laughed. "Why do you think?"

Blancanales squatted in front of them. "If you cooperate, you live."

The pro-fascist mercenaries looked to one another. The spotter spoke first.

"We don't get paid enough to die. What do you need to know?"

"Why the pictures of the president?" Lyons repeated.

"To hit that preacher."

"Unomundo intends to assassinate the president?"

The rifleman interrupted. "Mister, you're on the wrong side. Unomundo's going to kick ass *tomorrow*. As the man says, The New Reich Shall Rise."

14

Deep in the volcanic mountain, only their flashlights breaking the absolute night, they continued their questioning of the Nazi assassins. They squatted in a half-circle on a ledge. The cavern dome arched above them. Behind them, a chasm dropped into darkness.

"What happens tomorrow?" Lyons demanded.

"The Reich," the rifleman repeated. "Tomorrow we make a nation for all the dispossessed white people of the world. We will annihilate all the Commies and Christians, and start an empire of the strong and pure."

"Where are you from?" Blancanales asked him.

"Born in Texas. But I'm Rhodesian. Let me take you to Unomundo. He'll need men like you tomorrow. There's a place for you in the Reich. You'll live like princes."

"What happens tomorrow?" Lyons asked him again.

"There's still time to join. We leave after dark for the capital, my spotter and me. We're going to grease El Presidente Preacher in the morning when he goes out to pray. Our squads will kill the politicos in their beds. Then the gunships and airborne teams will hit the government buildings and the army garrisons.

Then buses and trucks will roll in with troops to secure the city.''

Lyons led them on. ''What kind of money can we get up front?''

''A few thousand. The real payoff comes after the victory, when we divide up the country. Everybody gets an estate. And money. And Indians as slaves. And the Indian girls for whores. How does that compare with a salary and a pension after thirty years?''

''You think he'd hire us, even after we killed the men up there?''

''Positive. You killed losers. He needs men like you. Untie us and we'll take you to him.''

''Right now? We could talk to him tonight?''

''Right now. He's briefing the commanders. And he'll be going in with the gunships tomorrow. He's no bigmouth lying politician, sending us to die, then rubbing bellies with the niggers and Commies. He'll lead his army from the front. Let's go! Right now. You can be on the winning side for a change.''

Taking his partners aside, Lyons asked them: ''We got enough from these monsters? I'm throwing them in that hole.'' He flicked a rock into the darkness of the chasm. Seconds later, far, far below, they heard the rock strike stone.

''Maybe they know where Unomundo is in the compound,'' Blancanales suggested. ''Then we hit him with that Walther rifle.''

Nate shook his head. ''The officers' quarters don't face out. There is no clear shot. My way is better. I will kill them all at once.''

''You got the plastic?'' Gadgets asked. ''We only brought a kilo of C-4 and some radio detonators.''

"It is there."

"You said the munitions are in another cave," Lyons reminded Nate.

"They are. Listen. I wanted to do this alone. But together we must do it tonight. I will contact my friends. A few men."

"Who are they?" Blancanales asked.

"Friends. Guatemalans. But I take the Nazis. They are mine. One hundred thousand dollars and two Nazis. Very cheap."

"But where's your explosive?" Gadgets asked him.

"In the cave. They have a five-hundred-gallon tank of propane—"

"Righteous!" Gadgets laughed with excitement. "If the conditions are right, that's better than TNT. You got my vote."

Lyons handed Nate his silenced Colt. "No torture session. We don't have the time."

"All I need is rope."

Nate returned to the two tied Nazis.

"What are you doing?" the rifleman demanded to know. "Man, you're an American, don't you—"

Cinching their gags tight, Nate stopped the talk. He kicked the pro-fascists onto their stomachs. Untying the nylon cords around their necks, he triple-tied their wrists behind their backs, then linked the two men by all the remaining rope, perhaps forty feet. As he worked, he pronounced sentence on them.

"You are not animals, you are not insects. You are less than shit. You are poison. You have poisoned this beautiful place with your European sickness. Eight years I lived here in peace. Now you come with slavery and death. My wife is Indian. My son is Indian. My friends are Indian. If there is a hell, I send you there. But first, you know hell here—''

Blancanales slipped out his Beretta. As he clicked off the safety to give the prisoners the mercy of a quick death. . . .

Nate looped the rope over a jutting rock and kicked the Nazis off the ledge. In the unnatural quiet of the volcanic chambers, they heard the Nazis' arms pop backward out of their shoulder sockets when the rope snapped taut.

They heard the guttural choking and thrashing of the gagged Nazis. Nate shouted down to them.

"It will take a week for you to die. When your arms rot off, you fall."

"Oh, wow," Gadgets sighed. "That one's straight out of a nightmare. Think they'll live a week?"

Lyons and Blancanales said nothing as Nate assembled his equipment. Below, the choking and thrashing continued. Finally, Lyons went to Nate.

He spoke softly as he slipped out a knife. "We're not like them. No matter what they do, we're not them."

"That is how they killed Xagil's father. The husband of my wife's sister. For them to suffer is justice."

"No, it's only revenge. And if we stop to avenge every murder, every atrocity, they will take the world. It is not victory to torture the torturers."

Lyons cut the rope. A moment later, the Nazis smashed on the rocks.

None of them spoke. Nate turned away. Able

Team followed him through the maze of the mountain's interior.

TWO HOURS LATER, they returned to the sanctuary of the cave overlooking the valley. Nate dispatched Xagil to gather the men from hidden farms scattered throughout the mountains.

"I told him to run," Nate reported to Able Team "but it will be hours before they all come. Now we plan the attack."

Drawing with charcoal on the wood of his handmade table, the expatriate Nam vet sketched the complex of barracks and equipment yards. A tiny helicopter indicated the scale of the vast cavern of Unomundo.

"It faces east." Nate pointed to each position "Here, they have three levels of pre-fab bunkhouses Here and here, where the ceiling is high, they put down the helicopters."

Lyons interrupted. "And that's where Unomundo lands his helicopter?"

"Always."

"Does he have bodyguards?"

"Always. His soldiers. Traitors from the Guatemalan army."

"Does he have his own helicopter? Or just one of their gray Hueys?"

"It is blue and white. Like a company helicopter."

"We can't do anything unless we're sure he's in the cave," Lyons told his partners. "If we kill only his people, he can buy more. I'm asking about the bodyguards and helicopter because I want to hit him first We've got to get him if—"

Blancanales stopped Lyons. "Let's get the details. Nate, please continue."

"They park heavy equipment and trucks on the north side. The passage to the cave where they store the munitions goes through the north side.

"In the west end of the cave, there is a mess hall and rec area. The propane is behind the mess hall. Once we get to the tank, no one will see us. No one can see it where it is. But there will be many guards. You know how a propane bomb works?"

"Oh, yeah," Gadgets told him. "In Nam, they'd use it to neutralize landing zones. Drop a fifty-gallon tank of it into the jungle, give the stuff time to spread out, then a time-delay fuse sets it off. Just like detcord and napalm wrapped around a thousand trees going off all at once. Turned jungles into parking lots. Except if we had wind, that would—"

Nate nodded. "But there won't be wind tonight from midnight until dawn."

"Are you positive?" Lyons demanded.

"I live here. I know the weather. I have planned this for months. I am positive. What we must do is get in there quiet, close the main valve, wait, then hacksaw the line. After that we try to get out. We cannot shoot on the way out—"

"If we want to live through it," Gadgets concluded for him.

"Why close the valve first?" Lyons asked.

Gadgets filled in some technical details. "Like a pilot light on a kitchen stove. If the gas only goes a small distance before it catches, no blast. Just a fire. We want the gas everywhere in the cave before it goes. This man's given us a great way to fix those

Nazis. Short of zipping a missile in there, this is it."

"What about cigarettes?" Blancanales asked. "Someone in the cave or bunkhouse is going to be smoking."

"A cigarette won't ignite propane," Gadgets continued. "Has to be a flame. Or C-4—"

Nate pointed to the sketch. "The bunkhouses are raised up from the rock. Three feet, some places six feet."

"Liquid petroleum gas isn't like natural gas." With enthusiasm, Gadgets took over Nate's plan. "Natural gas is lighter than air. Propane is heavier than air, and it'll be cold. It'll stay down for a few minutes, then start to dissipate. We'll put two doses of C-4 plastic on the tank, with radio-triggers. A main charge and a backup."

"My friends will be outside," Nate continued. "It would be a miracle if the blast killed every Nazi."

"Right," Lyons agreed. "We'll throw a circle of rifles around the loading area. Plus we've got that rifle with the Starlite scope—"

"My Heckler & Koch," Gadgets interrupted. "I've carried it long enough. Time to use it again."

"And the Walther?" Lyons meant the Walther .300 Magnum sniping rifle captured from the Nazi assassins.

"No," Blancanales shook his head. "If you're going into the cave, we'll be carrying your equipment. Your armor, bandoliers, grenades. Can't carry that weapon."

"But for any of them that get out of the cave..." Lyons suggested. "We'll need to knock them down with rifle fire."

"At that distance," Blancanales answered, "the M-16s will do it. That Walther, the range increments start at three hundred yards."

"Yeah, you're right."

Gadgets jived him. "Don't cry, Ironman. Take the space gun home as a souvenir."

Nate stopped their laughter. "Here is a problem. Other than us four, I have only two men who can hit a running target. All my friends are brave, and they have served in the Civil Guard, but they don't have enough training."

As the hours passed in discussion of small details and contingencies, the men from the village and farms joined them, arriving one and two at a time. Every man carried an M-16 and a machete. Like Nate, they carried their grenades and spare magazines in hand-knitted bags. Instead of captured fatigues, they wore traditional clothes: embroidered peasant pants, bright colored shirts, coats of black wool, all hand-woven and embroidered.

Lyons stopped the planning. "Nate, those men need uniforms."

"We know what to wear," Nate told him. "You think we should all wear Unomundo's uniforms? You want us to face our god wearing rags stolen from Nazi soldiers?"

"This isn't some kind of religious expedition," Lyons protested. "We're going into a night attack. And you, you're talking about going into the complex."

"Okay, I'll be wearing the gray uniform. But they wear what they want."

Nate's Mayan wife bathed his wound. After Blancanales applied a sterile dressing, Marylena bound the dressing with a length of hand-embroidered cloth. She helped him slip a gray shirt over the cloth.

"Dig it, Ironman," Gadgets commented. "The cloth is magic. Like genipap and jockstraps—"

Flipping open his wallet, Gadgets took out a dog-eared snapshot taken in the Bolivian Amazon. He gave it to Nate.

"That's the Ironman wearing his magic."

Nate looked at the photo, then at the blond ex-cop across the table. The snapshot showed Lyons wearing only a loincloth, a pistol belt, and bandoliers. Sandals protected his feet. His hair had been cut into a bowl. Blacking covered his entire body except at the shoulders, where two patches of red paint added brilliant color.

Laughing, Nate passed the snapshot to his wife. She stared. She looked at Lyons. Her sister leaned over her shoulder. They both laughed. Xagil took the photo and laughed. He ran across the cave to the knot of Indian men. In seconds, everyone in the cave laughed.

Nate went to the other men. He talked with them as they gathered their gear. A bottle of clear liquor went from man to man.

"Time to move, spooks," Nate told Able Team. He offered the bottle to them. *"Aguardiente."*

Lyons shook his head. Nate pushed the bottle into his hand.

"Drink. You are part of a very important occasion. Tonight we free Azatlan from Unomundo."

Gadgets took the bottle and gulped. Then he gulped air as he passed the bottle to Lyons. "It's only alcohol," he gasped. "About a hundred proof. But it ain't a drug. No super snuff on this trip. Last time Ironman participated in an Indian ritual, he got psychedelicized. And indigenized. But don't be afraid, take a swallow."

Lyons finally drank, then passed the bottle to Blancanales.

The appearance of a bloody young man stopped the laughter. He talked quickly in Quiche with Nate and the other men.

"Oh, God, not alive," Nate groaned. Then he translated for Able Team. "Unomundo mercenaries ambushed his brother and uncle. He thinks they were taken alive. We must hurry. Perhaps we can end their suffering."

15

ELECTRONICS GUIDED THE FIGHTERS—Guatemalan and North American—through the cool moonlit darkness of the forest. Nate and Lyons walked point. Lyons held the Atchisson ready, a 12-gauge shell in the chamber, his thumb on the safety. Nate carried the H&K MP 5 silenced submachine gun, using the Starlite scope to penetrate the night Knowing every trail and hill, every smell and sound of the valley of Azatlan, the ex-Marine rarely needed the Starlite's light-enhancing optics.

Gadgets followed with the Indians. Able Team's communications specialist also scanned the night with electronics—but not in the visual spectrum. He monitored the several frequencies used by the pro-fascist mercenaries, listening for the chatter of squads on patrol or the clicks of ambush units. He walked almost deaf, wearing two earphones. One went to the altered circuits of a merc walkie-talkie, the other to the hand-radio linking him to Lyons and Blancanales. Able Team did not fear the monitoring of their frequency. Sophisticated encoding circuits totally scrambled every transmission.

Blancanales walked at the end of the line, his M-16/M-203 cocked and locked, a 40mm fragmentation round in the grenade tube. In case of action or ambush, he would need to serve as a radioman and translator. Only Nate spoke English, Spanish and Quiche. The Indians spoke Quiche and some Spanish. Gadgets spoke very little Spanish, Lyons almost none. Only Lyons, Gadgets, and Blancanales had radios. The combinations and permutations of languages threatened the group with communications chaos. And in combat, failure to communicate often meant death.

Descending the rocky slopes, they saw the lights of trucks moving on the dirt road. They moved quickly down the slope, Nate leading the group across untraveled ground. He acccpted the slight sounds of their legs moving through ferns, the soft crackling of their feet on the woodland mulch, rather than risk ambush on the trails.

They entered the trees. With the branches screening the moonlight, they now walked in total darkness. The line closed up, each man putting a hand on the shoulder of the man ahead. Only Nate, with the Starlite, had sight. He scanned the black from time to time to spot the trees and obstacles ahead, then walked through the darkness by memory.

As they neared the road, Lyons saw lights again, streaking toward him from the darkness like tracers or distant headlights. He flinched, then realized he had not heard a shot or a truck.

"What?" Nate whispered. He had felt Lyons's hand startle on his shoulder.

"Lights. I see. . .there! A light."

"Fireflies, spook man."

At the road, they went flat on the earth. Nate watched the tree lines with the Starlite scope. Gadgets monitored the mercenary frequencies. But they did not have time to wait for a mercenary unit to betray itself with movement or careless talk or a cigarette.

Nate turned to Lyons and pointed across the road. Then the ex-Marine went to two of his Quiche friends and whispered for them to follow the North American. When no autofire or Claymores cut down the first three men, more followed.

At the opposite tree line, Lyons crouched in the darkness. He knew the extreme danger the others faced as they crossed. An ambush unit would not hit the first few men. They would wait until the road divided the North Americans and Indians into two groups, then hit them both. Retreat would divide their group. Advance meant sacrificing men in the kill zone.

Fireflies and the cries of nightbirds teased Lyons' reactions. His eyes strained to find form or movement around them. His ears heard the boots and sandals of his companions on the gravel. Calming his breathing, he sucked down long, smooth breaths through his nose. He smelled only the pines and the dry grass and his own two-day odor.

Vibrations under his feet warned him. He keyed his hand-radio and whispered. "Truck coming."

Clicks answered. Then a voice sounded in the earphone he wore. "We're all across."

They moved into the trees. Hearing gravel rattle in fenders and the squeak of springs, they went flat as headlights came over a rise.

A bus passed them. More headlights, another bus. Then a flatbed stake-sided truck. The truck's headlight glare lit the interior of the second bus. They saw a gray-uniformed mercenary driving. A second mercenary stood in the door, his M-16 pointed into the night.

Blancanales and Lyons heard Gadgets whisper through their earphones.

"Like the Nazi in the cave said, trucks and buses. To take the Nazi soldiers to Guatemala City."

They answered with clicks, then moved again.

Jogging through the darkness, Lyons thought of the irony and desperation of this night. With Quiche Indian men whose names he did not know, whose language he did not speak, he went to fight Nazis. A few men against a thousand. A few North Americans and Guatemalans against an army of pro-fascist mercenaries—North American felons, Central American murderers, criminals from England and France and Germany—killing in order to impose a murderous, racist regime on the beautiful nation of Guatemala.

Carl Lyons, the blond North American, had come full circle from his European ancestry. His forefathers had fought and decimated the Indian nations so that they could impose their European culture on the New World. Now, only two hundred years later, he fought with Indians as allies against another invasion. Americans—Anglo and Quiche—fighting European dogma and hatred. . . .

EMERGING FROM THE CAVERN, they heard the screams. Nate had led them through the labyrinth of passages and vast echoing chambers in a few minutes. This time they did not look down at the flat assembly area outside the hidden complex. They came out in the crevices and jumbled rocks level with the cave mouth. Only two hundred yards away, they saw the headlights of trucks. The glare of worklights from the huge cave lit the trees beyond the assembly area.

The screams tore the night. All of the fighters—North American and Guatemalan—heard them. Nate went to all the Indian men and whispered to them. Then he explained to the three men of Able Team:

"I told them we can do nothing for the captives Nothing until we blow the cave behind them. They must close their eyes and ears until then. And you, too."

When they planned the assault, Nate had briefed them on the terrain and security surrounding the complex. Because the four North Americans had the most training and experience, Nate and Able Team led the approach to the perimeter, the Quiche fighters following.

A cleared perimeter surrounded the complex. For a hundred yards around the truck park, only tree stumps remained of the forest. The grass had been burned to denude the earth. Mines and booby traps prevented intruders from crossing the perimeter.

The road wound around the mountain to approach the complex from the west. Trucks and buses passed a guardpost at the tree line, then continued up the slope to the complex.

As the group crept through the forest, Gadgets stopped. Signaling his Able Team partners with three clicks of his hand-radio, he halted the group. He whispered into his hand-radio

"Ambush."

Lyons grabbed Nate to stop him. Flat on the

ground, he hissed: "Ambush. Wizard caught it on the walkie-talkie."

"Need the Starlite?"

"Come on."

Lyons and Blancanales snaked over to their electronics specialist. Nate followed a moment later. They met in a tight knot, their heads touching, their whispers lost in the noise of the trucks only a hundred feet away.

"Where?" Blancanales hissed.

"Don't know. One merc radioed another."

"They hear us?" Lyons asked. "See us?"

"No. One checked with the other. A wake-up call. Could be on the other side of the road."

"Here's the Starlite." Nate passed the silenced MP-5 to Gadgets. "Signal us when." Nate crawled back to the Indians to halt them.

Gadgets flicked on the Starlite's power. Lyons felt his partner lay the Heckler & Koch submachine gun across his back. Gadgets swept the darkness with the electronics.

"Can't see.... Grass is too high and they've got cover. Not moving."

Able Team considered the options in silence. Wait? Retreat? Risk it?

"A rock," Lyons decided.

"Stay low," Gadgets cautioned him. "We could be in the kill zone right now."

Easing over on his back, Lyons searched through the grass and forest leaves for stones. He piled a handful on his stomach.

Tossing a pebble toward the road, he hit a tree fifty feet away. He waited, listening.

"Another one," Gadgets whispered.

The second stone pattered on leaves. Gadgets whispered again.

"Ten feet to the right this time."

The next rock bounced on stone. "One merc's telling the others to stop throwing rocks at him. Throw to the left."

A clink.

"Quit it!" a voice called out in English.

"What?" another voice answered.

"The rocks, you shit."

"I didn't throw any—"

"Estúpidos, silencio!"

Slipping out his silenced autoColt, Lyons crawled toward the voices. Blancanales shrugged off his backpack of gear and weapons, and followed. They moved infinitely slowly, gently pushing through the grass, advancing a few inches at a time. Minutes passed as they snaked closer and closer to where the pro-fascists hid in the darkness.

Blancanales heard a man shift positions in front of him, a boot squeaking, a buckle scraping across the metal of a rifle. He flicked his eyes back and forth, trying to find the man's form with the edges of his vision.

Only five feet away, the luminous numbers of a watch appeared. Twenty feet away, another man cleared his throat. Blancanales continued forward, feeling the ground ahead of him with his left hand, the Beretta in his right.

The man to his side cleared his throat again. Blancanales heard a boot scrape on a rock a mere arm's reach away from him.

A slap, like a fist against flesh, startled the man in front of him. The noise had come from where Lyons had gone. Blancanales heard the man click a walkie-talkie's transmit key, then whisper:

"What was that?"

A bullet through the brain answered him. The walkie-talkie clattered from the dead man's hand. Blancanales picked up the small radio and listened.

"Meyers?" A voice asked.

Blancanales hissed a reply. "Yeah?"

"Devlin here. Lupo?" The voice asked.

"Here." A Spanish accented voice answered.

"Cole?"

"Yeah?" Another hissed answer. Lyons.

A roll call. Three men and their leader. Two already dead.

On the road, a bus neared the guard post. An out-of-line headlight flashed through the trees. Blancanales saw the silhouette of the next man in the ambush unit. He braced his Beretta on the corpse in front of him. He lined up the dash-dot-dash of his Beretta's betalight nightsights, and waited.

As the next buses came up the road, dust diffusing the highbeams, Blancanales snapped two shots into the silhouette. One of the ejected casings clinked on a rock. He waited.

A hideous wavering scream came from the parked trucks.

Guffaws came from the darkness. "Listen to 'em fuckin' up those peons," said a muttered voice.

Blancanales pointed his Beretta at the voice and sprayed the lone laughing Nazi mercenary with a three-round burst. Two rounds slapped flesh, one slug skipped off stone and hit a tree.

The laughter became a gasp. Blancanales fired another burst, heard a bullet strike plastic and flesh. He fired again. He heared blood gurgle in a throat.

Then he picked up the walkie-talkie and whispered:

"Meyers?" No answer.

"Lupo?" No answer.

"Cole?" No answer.

"Devlin?" No answer.

He whispered into his hand-radio. "Wizard. Anything?"

"There's an ambush unit on the other side of the road. Using another frequency."

Lyons broke in. "Forget them. The road."

Signalling Nate and the Indians forward, the group crawled a hundred feet to the road. They reassembled opposite the guard post.

Two mercenaries manned the post, their M-16 rifles slung over their shoulders. As each bus or truck passed, they pointed their flashlights at the drivers then waved them past. Most of the drivers did no slow for the inspection.

Able Team sighted their silenced pistols on the two mercs. Nate aimed the MP-5. A bus sputtered pass the two mercs. Blancanales watched the road. He saw no headlights downslope.

"Now!"

Slugs punched into the mercs' heads and chests staggering them back with impacts.

As they fell, Gadgets and Blancanales dashed across to them and picked up the flashlights. Lyons and Nate followed. Still no headlights downhill. Nate waved the Indians across.

Gadgets and Blancanales manned the guard post.

A truck approached. Blancanales stepped out into the road, waving his flashlight. As the truck slowed, he put the beam on the gray-uniformed driver. Blancanales stepped back out of the road.

The truck shifted, the engine revved, then it continued up the road, regaining speed.

Lyons and Nate rode the truck's rear bumper to the cavern fortress of Unomundo.

16

LIKE THE YAWNING MOUTH OF A SKULL, the vast cavern exposed the interior of the mountain. Thousand-watt worklights illuminated the complex of barracks, offices, equipment yards and helipads. The mouth of the cavern opened to the east, exactly as Nate had described.

On the south end, prefabricated steel barracks rose three stories from the concrete and naked stone of the cave floor. Other steel buildings clustered at the west end where the ceiling of the cavern curved down. A concrete wall sealed the west end from the maze of passages and chambers within the volcanic mountain.

On the north end, steel aircraft hangars served as workshops for mechanics and welders. Trucks and two bulldozers lined the north wall.

In the center, where the arcing dome of the cavern created a two-hundred-foot-high airspace between the floor and the apex, Cobra gunships and Huey troop carriers waited for the next day's assault. Mechanics and ordnance technicians moved from helicopter to helicopter, servicing the engines, loading the multi-million-dollar weapon systems.

Lyons and Nate stood in the back of a stake-bed truck, surveying the fortress and the army of the Nazi warlord. Trucks and buses parked around them, mercenaries driving the vehicles to the wide, flat parking area scraped from the hills. Mercenaries walked past the truck where they stood without giving the two men a glance. With their European faces and gray uniforms, the two infiltrators passed as Nazis.

Beyond the gravel area, a hundred yards of scorched hillside separated the base from the forest. Only the road breached the perimeter.

Lyons squatted in the shadows with his hand-radio.

"Ironman speaking. We're in. There's no other way in but the road."

"Won't be a problem," Blancanales responded.

"The trucks and buses enter and park in rows. No one checks the interiors. No sentries. A few mercs wandering around. Everyone else is busy. . . ."

A scream, then laughter came from the center of the parking area. Lyons and Nate could not see the scene of torture from the truck where they surveyed the complex. But the screams told them of the terror and suffering. Lyons took one of the radio-fused charges from under his gray fatigue shirt and passed it to Nate. Now they each had a pound of C-4 plastic explosive hidden under their belts.

"Wizard," Lyons whispered into his radio.

"Here. Nothing crazy yet. Monitoring it all."

"You're not hearing what I'm hearing. Do us a favor. If they take us, push the button on the radio charges. Understand?"

"Understand. Over and adios, brother."

Blancanales's voice came on. "Nate. Ironman. Good luck."

Lyons clicked off. Nate dropped to the gravel. Lyons followed a moment later. They walked through the vehicles, double-checking for sentries. In the shadows and glaring lights, pro-fascist mercenaries passed Nate and Lyons. But their uniforms and weapons concealed them. Still, Nate kept his left hand near the pistol grip of his M-16. He kept his right arm tucked into his belt, only six inches from a holstered Colt Government Model on full-cock. Lyons folded his arms over his Atchisson to conceal the oversized receiver group and magazine. He had seen mercenaries carrying G-3s, Galils and Remington 870s. Though he did not fear that the Atchisson would betray him, he did not want mercenaries to question him about his avant-garde full-auto assault shotgun.

A six-foot-high chain link fence marked the edge of the mine field. Signs marked with a skull and crossbones and printed in four languages—English, Spanish, French and German—warned the camp personnel of the danger. Lyons and Nate started to the cavern.

When they left the parked buses and trucks, they saw the horror.

Truck headlights lit the scene. In the center of the large graveled area for the trucks, steel beams leaned against the platform of a cargo truck. Chains bound the young man and his uncle to the beams. A mercenary with a welding torch played the intense blue flame over the blackened stumps of the older Indian's legs, the man's feet and ankles already burned away.

The night stank of scorched flesh.

Other mercenaries crowded around, laughing and guzzling booze. As Nate and Lyons approached, another torturer heated a steel rod red hot. Then he jammed it into one of the boy's eyes.

The image and the scream tearing through his consciousness, Lyons staggered, dizzy with horror and sorrow, his gut knotting. He stumbled, Nate catching him.

As the fascists a few steps away laughed at the nightmare, Lyons dropped to his hands and knees and vomited. Nate knelt beside him, his good left arm over Lyons's shoulder as he gasped and choked. Nate felt a sob wrack the North American.

"Can't keep that booze down, eh, man?"

"Take a drink," said a voice.

Nate looked up. A drunken mercenary held out a pint bottle of *aguardiente*. He took it. "Thanks."

"Tonight a party," the mercenary laughed, twisting off the cap of another bottle. "But tomorrow, the orgy starts."

The guy moved on. Nate offered the bottle to Lyons. Around them, mercenaries looked at the blond man staring into his vomit, then turned back to the spectacle of the Indians.

"Drink, they're looking at us."

Lyons's hand moved for the grip of his Atchisson. Nate grabbed his arm and held it tight. He whispered to Lyons:

"Don't see it. There's nothing we can do. They're done for. But, they would understand. They know we're here, but they've said nothing. Therefore they know they'll not die for nothing. We are going to walk past, and then we are going to burn this monster. If we can do it quick, they'll survive long enough to know it. Let's do it before they die."

Nodding, wiping his face, Lyons stood. He gulped from the bottle and staggered. As they passed the horror, Lyons looked again.

Lyons was no longer broken by the crime. Nate saw a face that had become stone, although it was streaked with tears. The sparking and popping of the welding torch lit his hardened features as Lyons looked at the scene, and scorched the image into his mind forever.

They walked toward the cave. Pouring *aguardiente* into his hand, Lyons washed his face with the high-proof alcohol. He brushed back his short hair. Nate heard Lyons's breath shuddering in his throat.

For the first time, Nate trusted this stranger who fought with him and his Quiche friends.

"You know how I came here?" Nate spoke suddenly, his voice as loud as the other mercenaries walking around them. "You must think Guatemala is no-where. When I was eighteen, I was a badass Marine Recon warrior dropping into Laos. Had some severe personality conflicts with my commander. We did not agree on what was acceptable human behavior with prisoners and non-combatants."

As they approached the mercenaries working in the cave, Nate lowered his voice. "I liked those people. I wish we'd won the war, I wanted to stay there. In-stead, my commander got shot in the back one mission. I get convicted of shooting him, Murder Two. Life in Leavenworth."

"Did you shoot him?" Lyons asked.

"I don't know. Maybe. Things get confused when

you have a People's Army battalion chasing you through the jungle.''

The two men entered the cave. They passed unchallenged through the preparations for the next day's coup. In the center of the cavern, parked among the Cobras and Hueys, they saw a blue-and-white executive helicopter.

"Is that his?" Lyons asked.

"I've seen it before. But. . . ."

Walking along the side of the three-story barracks, they scanned the officers of the command staff. They saw plainclothes guards standing at the doors of one office.

"His men?" Lyons asked.

"All the Guatemalan and Salvadoran fascists have bodyguards."

"You break out of Leavenworth?" Lyons had to know.

"Out of a prison bus. Two other prisoners had friends ambush the bus on the highway. I'd done two years in the brig while the trials and appeals went on, and I knew what to expect in Leavenworth. I escaped with them. They took me to the Black Panthers and the Weatherman. I was the most qualified soldier that ever came their way. They wanted me to be a guerilla warfare instructor. To help them kill police. Politicians. I told them to stuff it. I went south. Through Mexico, into Guatemala, into the mountains. I had a good life, never wanted to go back. But Unomundo came."

Nate pointed behind the prefabricated mess hall and kitchens. They stepped off the concrete path. Maintaining an even, unhurried pace across the irregular stone of the cave floor, they walked behind the kitchens.

Stenciled red warnings marked the sides of a gleaming white cylinder.

DANGER
LIQUID PETROLEUM GAS
EXTREMELY INFLAMMABLE

This was what they sought. Lyons and Nate crawled along under the pipes and concrete blocks that supported the prefab units, then waited and watched. Footsteps crossed the floor of the mess hall, making the metal floor creak.

Only ten feet separated them from the one-inch galvanized pipes connecting the tank to the kitchen. They waited for a minute, then crawled to the pipe. It was dangerous; they were exposed to view.

Nate closed the emergency valve. He took the radio-fused slab of C-4 explosive from under his shirt and gave it to Lyons. He slipped a hacksaw blade from the bloodstained top of the gray boots he wore.

As Nate sawed on the pipe, Lyons moved back to snake himself under the tank. He put the first charge where the base brackets met the cylinder. Molding the puttylike explosive, he formed a strip along a foot of the tank's circumference. He came up on the far side of the tank. He found a valve welded into the end of the tank. A steel cap sealed off the valve. The second charge went around the weld. He could take his time because he was concealed from view.

"What the hell you doin', soldier?"

A cook stood on the walkway. The guy wiped his hands on his stained apron as he looked down at Nate. Lyons stayed flat on the rocks.

"Leak in the joint," Nate told him, pointing to the emergency valve.

"Where?"

"Here. You can smell it."

The gray-haired, overweight cook waddled over to the pipe. "I didn't notice anything."

Nate stood as the cook bent down to look.

"Hey, you're hacksawing the goddamned—"

Grabbing the mercenary's head by the ears, Nate slammed his head into the valve again and again, using the valve handle to crush his forehead. He shoved the body under the mess hall.

"Close," Lyons hissed.

"A few more minutes."

"Cut it. But don't open the valve yet. I want to confirm that he's here, right now, in the cave."

"How?"

"I'll do it." Lyons keyed his hand-radio. "Pol. Wizard. Charges are set. He's cutting the line. I'm going to go confirm on the man."

Blancanales answered. "Next bus, we're coming in."

Lyons left Nate sawing at the line. Forcing himself to walk slowly, his eyes swept the vast cavern for the blond, half-German Unomundo. At the executive helicopter, a Hispanic in a tailored Italian suit, gold flashing on his wrist and fingers, supervised the work of a crew of mechanics.

At the steps to the rows of offices, two well-dressed Hispanics with Uzis questioned a mercenary soldier. They would not let him pass. The mercenary shouted past them to one of the fascist leaders leaving an office: "His men won't let me go back to my office."

The mercenary from the office, his fatigues starched and pressed, a badge of rank on one shoulder, called down to the bodyguards: "That soldier's on the staff. He's authorized."

The bodyguard stood aside. Lyons realized that none of the mercenaries he saw on the office walkways carried weapons. He saw no M-16s, no side arms.

Lyons returned to the mess hall. Following the walkway past the kitchens, he saw that the rear of the building butted against the irregular stone of the cavern's south wall. He slipped into the dark space.

The shadows became darkness. He stumbled over pipes and scraps of wood and sheet metal. Light from office interiors shone through ventilator grilles.

A voice came from the ventilators of a second floor. The speaker raved in Spanish. Lyons damned his ignorance of the language. Yet he knew he heard Unomundo. The rhythms, the exclamations, the modulation of the tones indicated the professional rhetoric of a politician. But he had to confirm his guess.

At the end of the office building, he crossed to the barracks. He rushed to the end of the barracks walkway. Twenty feet away, the bodyguards stood at the steps to the offices.

Keeping his right hand on top of his Atchisson's receiver, his left hand in the open, Lyons jogged to them. Their eyes narrowed as the mercenary with the autoweapon rushed to them. Lyons saluted.

"Got a message for Unomundo. The *peones* are talking. They are part of a CIA plot. My officer continues the interrogation. Would our commander want to question the Indians?"

The Hispanics listened without speaking. One looked to the other, glanced toward the offices. The second man nodded, then ran up the stairs.

"Wait," the bodyguard told Lyons.

"I'll come back. I must get my colonel."

Flashing another salute, Lyons jogged to the mess hall. He glanced back. The bodyguard watched him. He went around the corner to the kitchens. He saw no one in the area. In a few seconds, he squatted beside Nate.

"He's here."

Only a fraction of a centimeter of steel linked the two sections of pipe. Nate grabbed the valve and wobbled it, attempting to break the pipes apart. Lyons kicked the pipe, once, twice, stood on it and jumped.

The pipe broke. Lyons spoke into his hand-radio.

"We've cut the line. And we've confirmed Unomundo's here. Are you ready?"

"Affirmative," Blancanales answered. "We're in. The men are moving into position."

"This is it. Over."

Nate opened the valve. A colorless gas rushed from the severed pipe. Looking through the spreading gas, they saw the shadowy rocks waver as the flow spread. White frost formed instantly on the valve and pipe and the rocks.

Lyons and Nate ran. At the mess hall walkway, they forced themselves to slow to a quick walk. Lyons pointed to the center of the complex.

They strode toward the helicopters. Lyons looked back once at the offices. Bodyguards, pro-fascist mercenaries and Guatemalan army officers—the traitors' chests bright with medals—crowded from a door. All the Nazis attempted to speak with one person, a tall, blond man with the sharp sculpted features of an aristocrat. Wide-shouldered bodyguards knotted around him.

"Unomundo," Lyons told Nate.

Nate glanced back at him and smiled. "Soon he burns in hell."

A bodyguard spoke with Unomundo. The Hispanic pointed into the night to the searing light of the welding torch torturing the two Quiche men. Unomundo spoke with a mercenary officer. The officer led Unomundo and a knot of bodyguards down the steps.

Lyons and Nate maintained their stride. They passed Hueys and Cobras. Technicians loaded rocket pods. Other men pumped aviation fuel into the helicopters' tanks. Nate smiled to Lyons.

Leaving the brilliant light of the cavern, they saw a flashlight blink from the top of a parked bus.

The crowd of drunken mercenaries laughed. A scream rose, wavered, faded. Lyons's hand-radio buzzed.

"Give the signal!" Gadgets told him, his voice seething with anger and frustration. "Time to put that goon gang down!"

The rotorthrob of a helicopter approached from the sky. With his thumb on the transmit key, Lyons looked up at the black silhouette of a Huey against the stars. He looked back to Unomundo.

Leaving the cavern, Unomundo and his bodyguards hurried to the horror. The Hispanic bodyguard who had listened to the faked message about the CIA and the Indians pointed to Lyons. Unomundo and all the bodyguards turned.

Lyons hissed into the hand-radio. "Wizard, do it! He's getting out!"

Swinging the barrel of his Atchisson around, Lyons flicked down the safety and sprayed full-auto high-velocity steel at the Nazi warlord.

A great wave of flame churned from the cavern.

17

A ROAR CAME, then heat, but no explosion. Uncompressed and too cold to mix with the air, thus lacking the correct oxygen-to-gas ratio, the liquid petroleum gas—unlike a true explosive—failed to flash instantaneously into the heat and combustion wastes. Yet the gas had spread under and beyond the kitchen and mess hall areas, to the command offices, and to the barracks and the helicopters.

In the first milliseconds of the fire, half the cavern was enveloped in a single flame. The initial instant of fire heated the inches-thick layer of cold gas that coated the floor of the cavern, causing the unburned gas to expand rapidly into the flames. As the heat of the flames accelerated the rate of combustion, and the heat produced churning air currents that intermixed the flames and expanding gas with more oxygen, the flames rose still higher. This happened in the first fifteen-hundredths of a second after Gadgets Schwarz detonated the radio-fused plastic explosive.

The exploding charge also tore open the steel tank that held hundreds more gallons of liquid gas. Encountering the superheated atmosphere, the fuel expanded into gas. In the absence of oxygen—the available atmospheric oxygen had been consumed by the first flash of flame—the unburned gas surged outward. When it mixed with the atmosphere, it also flamed.

Though the Nazi personnel did not suffer dismemberment, all of the personnel in the south half of the cave received instantaneous third-degree burns. Then the wave of flame enveloped the helicopters and aviation fuel.

Av-gas became superheated. It burned, radiating a flash-temperature of three thousand degrees Centigrade. Every combustible object or substance— wood, hoses, insulated wires, tires, fuel, clothing, hair, skin fat—burst into flame.

In the center of the flames, the staff offices became the crematorium of the Nazi commanders and the handful of Guatemalan army officers who had betrayed their country to Unomundo's European doctrine.

The hired commandos sleeping in the steel barracks knew a few seconds of confusion and agony as they woke to red hot walls and superheated air. When they screamed at the shock of their waking nightmare, they scorched their lungs, and died choking seconds later. As the flames and heat continued, the glowing barracks baked the dead men's bodies. Fat flowed and burned, contributing to the inferno.

Mercenaries and technicians in the open felt only an instant of pain before their bodies became ash.

Outside, a few of the mercenaries near the mouth of the cavern turned to the roar. The heat-flash melted their faces. Others threw themselves down. Those near the fire received third-degree burns, their uniforms first smoking, then bursting into flame.

Unomundo sprawled under the corpses of three of

his bodyguards. Stunned by a head wound caused by a .33-caliber steel ball that had punched through the head of one of his bodyguards to tear through his own left cheek and ear, Unomundo saw the diffused glare of the inferno. He did not suffer burns. The bodies of his guards had saved him. He heard screams, then autofire from a dozen rifles.

Knowing that his lifelong dream had been shattered only hours before he made it reality, he lay still. Now he plotted survival.

HEAT SEARING THEIR BACKS, Lyons and Nate sprinted into the shelter of the parked trucks and buses. A Quiche saw them, mistook them for mercenaries. As he raised his M-16, another Quiche knocked the rifle aside, a single shot ripping through the side of the bus.

"Get the Nazi clothes off, spookman!" Nate shouted at him over the screaming and shooting and the roar of the burning cavern complex. He ripped off his shirt to expose his light skin and bandage of red cloth.

"Politician!" Lyons called out.

"Your armor's up here!" Blancanales answered.

Climbing the side ladder to the cargo rack of a bus, he saw Blancanales on the bus roof, snapping single shots into Nazi mercenaries. Every shot killed. Blancanales sighted on two mercs dragging a burned comrade to the cover of a truck, and he triggered a 40mm grenade. Steel-wire shrapnel shredded the three.

"How many still alive?" Lyons yelled, going prone beside his partner. Blancanales had already discarded his own Nazi shirt. He wore his black battle armor and a red Indian shirt whose sleeves would identify him in the firefight.

"Maybe fifty, sixty. Most of the ones doing the torture, some drivers, some officers."

Lyons took grenades and his heavy Kevlar and steel trauma-plate battle armor from the pack. He stripped off his gray shirt, started to put on the armor. He found one of Nate's hand-sewn cotton shirts folded inside the armor, the cotton fabric woven in the design and color of Marylena's Quiche village.

"The shirt's for you," Blancanales told him. He touched the cloth of his own shirtsleeves. "Magic."

"With Kevlar and steel plates, it's magic."

"What about Unomundo?"

"Got him. Put him and his bodyguards down with a full-auto chop job," Lyons grinned. He slapped his Atchisson. "Lyons's Crowd Killing Device."

Lyons pulled on the red shirt, then the battle armor, and he watched the Huey troopship that hovered above the scene. The troopship stayed at a thousand feet, only observing.

Blancanales glanced at Lyons's new uniform— black armor, red sleeves pinstriped with yellow and purple, black nylon bandoliers and gray pants.

"No one's mistaking you for a Nazi, most definitely."

Gadgets came up the ladder. He also wore a red shirt under his armor. "Did we kill that Nazi?"

"The Ironman did."

"Where's the body?"

Lyons pointed. In the light of the inferno, he saw the tangled corpses of the bodyguards. "In that pile."

Blancanales jammed another 40mm round in the M-203 fitted under his M-16. "Now they die again."

The 40mm grenade hit one of the corpses. High-velocity steel tore the bodies a second time.

"War's over, gentlemen," Lyons told his partners. "Now it's payback and bodycount."

With a salute, he went down the ladder. His Atchisson cocked and locked, his thigh pockets heavy with grenades, he jogged between the rows of vehicles, searching for targets.

The body of a mercenary lay in the narrow walk-space. Point-blank autofire had killed him, then machetes had dismembered the torso. At the end of the bus, an Indian fired quick bursts from his M-16. Lyons neared him and called out:

"Qui-chay, qui-chay." To identify himself, Lyons spoke the only word he knew of their language.

As he dropped out a spent magazine, the fighter nodded to Lyons. Slugs slammed into the sheet metal of the bus, windows broke above them as a mercenary sprayed auto-fire.

Taking cover behind the double rear wheels of the bus, Lyons dropped flat and peered under the frame. He saw a muzzle flash. More bullets tore through the bus.

The mercenary also had the shelter of heavy-duty wheels. Though return fire from the Indians had flattened the truck tires, the steel-belted rubber and the steel rims stopped the 5.56mm bullets from the M-16s. Lyons had a solution.

Konzaki had included two magazines of one-ounce steel-cored slugs with Lyons's 12-gauge ammunition. Dropping the magazine of shot shells out of his

Atchisson, he slapped in the magazine of slugs. Sighting on the muzzle flash, he fired three quick blasts.

The chambered shell sprayed the mercenary with double ought and Number Two steel shot. Then the Atchisson's bolt fed the first of the slugs into the chamber. Traveling 1,200 feet per second at four inches off the gravel, the first slug tore through the tire, then continued through the gunman's body. The second punched through the wheel to again rip the Nazi's body. The autofire stopped.

Dashing out, the Indian ran to the other side of the truck. Lyons followed. A burst of fire from the Indian's M-16 shattered the dead merc's skull.

Lyons and the Indian continued, covering one another as they ran from walkspace to walkspace. They passed an Indian with a bullet-torn arm. He sat against a truck wheel, binding the wound with a strip of cloth. Lyons paused to check the man's injury for arterial bleeding. Despite the pain, the Indian smiled and waved Lyons past.

Indians fired at the two trucks in the center of the parking area. The two tortured men still lay on the steel beams. In two groups, mercenaries clustered behind the protection of the trucks. Several autorifles flashed.

Lyons's hand-radio buzzed. "What goes?"

"One of them's radioing that helicopter," Gadgets told him. "Politician's listening now—"

Blancanales's voice came on the frequency. "Unomundo's still alive."

"What?"

"Wounded but alive. The helicopter's coming down for him."

A voice called out from trucks in Spanish. Nate shouted back. Lyons crept down the line of fighters to the North American ex-Marine.

"What do they want?" Lyons asked.

"They say our tortured men are still alive," Nate said. "They'll let them live if we let them go. Or they'll execute them."

"It's Unomundo—"

"I saw you shoot him."

"He's alive." Lyons pointed up at the Huey troopship. "He radioed the helicopter."

The voice called out again in Spanish. Nate listened. Then he spoke to his men in Quiche. The men moved position so they could see their mutilated friends.

One Indian called out in Quiche.

The blinded, scorched boy moved his head, and in a weak, quavering voice called back to his friends. The Indian shouted again. The boy answered, then lay back.

As one, the Quiche men raised their rifles and sighted. Autofire from ten rifles ripped the dying man and boy, ending their suffering.

Lyons jerked the pin from a fragmentation grenade and threw it past the trucks. A second grenade went under the nearest truck. As he pulled the cotter pin from a third grenade, shrapnel from the first one tore into the cowering mercenaries. The second punched steel through the truck's gas tank.

He threw the third, then a fourth grenade, and shouldered his autoshotgun. A mercenary ran from the flaming truck. He never reached the cover of the second truck. Sighting on the center of his back, Lyons fired.

A one-ounce slug threw the merc forward. Bullets from the Indians' rifles ripped the falling man. Exploding grenades spun the corpse again. The chaos of flames and flying shrapnel drove the other Nazis from cover.

Silhouetted against the flames of the complex that burned behind them, fascists sprinted in all directions. Autofire from the rifles of the Quiche men sprayed the running Nazis.

Rotorthrob drowned out the noise of the firefight. As the gray-painted Huey dropped from the stars, the door gunner strafed the buses and trucks. Glass shattered, slugs hammered steel, ricochets slammed into sheet metal.

"Nate!" Lyons shouted. "Spread them out. The helicopter's coming down for Unomundo."

Directing his friends in Quiche, Nate moved through the line, shoving men, pointing. Broken glass showered his back as he divided the men into groups. The men went to widely spaced positions along the lines of buses and trucks.

Dust that was orange with reflected flame swirled against the orange light of the blazing complex. Gravel pelted Lyons's face as he scanned the sprawled corpses and running men for the blond, fair-featured Unomundo. The Huey moved low along the scraped earth, the door gunner raking the vehicles.

A 40mm grenade missed. It exploded beyond the helicopter. The Huey spun and rose straight up. Tracers from an M-60 hammered the tops of several buses. Gasoline flamed. Autofire from the ground shattered the Plexiglas window of the Huey's side door.

Lyons sighted on the rectangle of the side door and fired a blast of steel shot. The tracers from the door gunner whipped about wildly, an orange line of unaimed slugs arcing into the sky. Lyons emptied the Atchisson, then slammed in the box mag of one-ounce slugs. He sighted on the Huey, and waited.

A body fell from the side door, then the M-60 fired again. Veering, swaying, the Huey came down again. Tracers from the door gun searched for the Quiche riflemen.

Following the pilot's windshield in his sights, Lyons fired. But the Huey troopship veered and swept across the parking area, its skids only ten feet from the gravel. Dust stormed around it. Light from the burning buses and trucks revealed the shadowy form of the helicopter in the dust. A line of tracers emerged.

Lyons fired again and again at the helicopter. The dust clouded like an orange wall, concealing the hovering bird.

As one, the surviving mercenaries fired their weapons at the Indians from behind the trucks.

Bullets punched metal above Lyons, then the fire stopped as the mercs dashed for the Huey.

Jumping from cover, Lyons sprinted across the open ground for the two trucks. A mercenary dropped the mag from his M-16, slammed in another before a one-ounce slug threw him back ten feet. Another raised a pistol. His head exploded in a spray of blood.

The Atchisson's action locked back. Lyons crouched against a bullet-dented fender as he dropped out his assault shotgun's empty magazine and shoved in another. He snapped a glance over the truck's hood, saw mercs grab the helicopter's skid. Lyons fired two blasts. A spray of steel severed a merc's arms.

Slugs screamed past his head. Throwing himself back, Lyons saw a merc pivot with an M-16 in his hands. Lyons zipped a blast of steel at the man. He saw the legs fly away from the torso. Lyons went to the fender again, and sighted on the helicopter.

The door gunner saw him. A line of tracers scythed the night as it sought Lyons.

Lyons pointed the Atchisson at the flashing muzzle of the machine gun only fifty feet away. He sprayed full-auto 12-gauge fire. The door gunner died. A mercenary fell back from the hovering helicopter. More Plexiglas showered from the side door. Then the whipping line of tracers, the M-60 still gripped in the dead hands of the gunner, found Lyons.

Lyons saw it as if in slow motion as he willed his body to move. The red line of tracers roared past him, hammering the truck. Slugs hit the shattered windshield, bits of glass flying, then fragments of the plastic dashboard exploded.

Slowed by his adrenalin-heightened perception, Lyons saw the flashing piece of metal and glass hurtling at him. He saw it coming, felt his body dropping though the air as he sought the shelter of the tires and gravel, then it hit him, the impact twisting him.

Lyons slammed into the gravel, his left arm numb. He grabbed for the wound, expecting to find his arm gone or a wound of shattered bone and gore. He felt no blood.

Then, on the gravel next to him, he saw what had

hit him: the bullet-warped steel and brilliant silver mosaic of a mirror from the truck.

Wounded by a rearview mirror!

His numb arm hanging, Lyons struggled to his feet. One-handed, he pointed the Atchisson. Beyond the hovering helicopter, a blond European-featured man in a suit ran for the other side door.

"Unomundo!" Lyons screamed, rushing the helicopter, his left arm dangling. With his right hand he fired the Atchisson twice. The action locked back, the weapon empty. Rifle fire flashed from behind him as Quiche men fired bursts at the fleeing mercenaries. Machetes flashed as they chopped wounded Nazis to pieces.

Fumbling with his bandolier, Lyons tried to change magazines one-handed and on the run. He saw Unomundo scramble up toward the Huey's far side door. Lyons could not reload the Atchisson. He threw the assault shotgun aside and pulled his Python.

As the helicopter lifted, he double-actioned slugs into the fuselage. The windshield shattered.

Lyons jumped. He tried to wrap his barely usable left arm around the skid. Blood-slick steel slipped from his failed grasp. Falling ten feet to the gravel, smashing down on his shoulder and side, Lyons rolled over and fired his Python at the underbelly of the Huey. The hammer finally fell on an empty chamber.

As the Indians slaughtered the last Nazi mercenaries with machetes and autofire, Lyons knew he had failed.

The monster Unomundo soared away. The Huey disappeared into the Guatemalan night.

For the first time, Able Team had lost their man. They had destroyed an evil dream, but they had not destroyed the mind that created it.

For the first time, Lyons truly understood what Mack Bolan meant by war everlasting.

Lyons would never rest until he had turned Unomundo's evil onto the monster himself. It might not happen next week, it might not happen next month, but eventually Carl Lyons would *do* Unomundo....

Dick Stivers, author of the Able Team series, was a
volunteer in Nam. He was too young to see the big
stuff there. His first major action was in the back
streets of Los Angeles during a mugging attempt; it
was his .22 against two Remingtons. Stivers won.
The popular, highly praised author is a world
traveler who has backpacked through many Central
and South American countries, most recently
haunting El Salvador. His ambition is to get rich
by writing great books.

ABLE TEAM

AN EXECUTIONER SERIES

#7 Justice by Fire

MORE GREAT ACTION COMING SOON!

It was death squad against death squad as Russian-backed, San Salvador-trained kill-groups hit the U.S. in a bizarre attempt to undermine our democracy. And dispatched to eliminate them...Able Team!

The death squads had been killing career criminals, psychopaths, political agitators—and thus they earned the gratitude of a public sick to death of the court's failures to punish rapists and murderers.

But, in fact, the vigilante squads were working for America's enemies. A crisis of democratic justice erupted, spilling out chaos.

Only Able Team can meet fire with fire, death with death.

Watch for new Able Team titles
wherever paperbacks are sold.

Mack Bolan's
ABLE TEAM

AN EXECUTIONER SERIES

by Dick Stivers

In the fire-raking tradition of The Executioner, Able Team's Carl Lyons, Pol Blancanales and Gadgets Schwarz are the three hotshots who avenge terror with screaming silvered fury. They are the Death Squad reborn, and their long-awaited adventures are the best thing to happen since the Mack Bolan and the Phoenix Force series. Collect them all! They are classics of their kind! Do not miss these titles!

"This guy has a fertile mind and a great eye for detail. Dick Stivers is brilliant!"

—*Don Pendleton*

#1 Tower of Terror   **#4 Amazon Slaughter**
#2 The Hostaged Island   **#5 Cairo Countdown**
#3 Texas Showdown   **#6 Warlord of Azatlan**

Able Team titles are available wherever paperbacks are sold.

GOLD EAGLE

Mack Bolan's

PHOENIX FORCE

AN EXECUTIONER SERIES

by Gar Wilson

Phoenix Force is The Executioner's five-man arm
that blazes through the dirtiest of encounters. Lik
commandos who fight for the love of battle and th
righteous unfolding of the logic of war, Bolan's fiv
hardasses make mincemeat out of their enemie
Catch up on the whole series now!

"Strong-willed and true. Gold Eagle Books are makin
history. Full of adventure, daring and action!"

—*Marketing Bestselle*

#1 Argentine Deadline	**#4 Tigers of Justice**
#2 Guerilla Games	**#5 The Fury Bombs**
#3 Atlantic Scramble	**#6 White Hell**

Phoenix Force titles are available
wherever paperbacks are sold.

GO
EAG

MACK BOLAN

I am not their judge, I am their judgment—I am their executioner.
—*Mack Bolan,*
a.k.a. Col. John Phoenix

Mack Bolan is the free world's leading force in the new Terrorist Wars, defying all terrorists and destroying them piece by piece, using his Vietnam-trained tactics and knowledge of jungle warfare. Bolan's new war is the most exciting series ever to explode into print. You won't want to miss a single word. Start your collection now!

"This is a publishing marvel. Stores have a hard time keeping these books in stock!"
—*The Orlando Voice*

#39 The New War
#40 Double Crossfire
#41 The Violent Streets
#42 The Iranian Hit
#43 Return to Vietnam
#44 Terrorist Summit
#45 Paramilitary Plot
#46 Bloodsport

#47 Renegade Agent
#48 The Libya Connection
#49 Doomsday Disciples
#50 Brothers in Blood
#51 Vulture's Vengeance
#52 Tuscany Terror
#53 The Invisible Assassins
#54 Mountain Rampage

GOLD
EAGLE

Available wherever paperbacks are sold.

HE'S EXPLOSIVE.
HE'S UNSTOPPABLE.
HE'S MACK BOLAN

He learned his deadly skills in Vietnam…then put them to use by destroying the Mafia in a blazing one-man war. Now **Mack Bolan** is back to battle new threats to freedom. the enemies of justice and democracy—and he's recruited some high-powered combat teams to help. **Able Team**—Bolan's famous D Squad, now reborn to tackle urban savagery too vicious for regular law enforcement. And **Phoenix Force**—five extraordinary warriors handpicked by Bolan to fight the dirtiest of anti-terrorist wars around the world.

Fight alongside these three courageous forces for freedom in all-new, pulse-pounding action-adventure novels! Travel to the jungles of South Ame the scorching sands of the Sahara and the desolate mountains of Turkey. And feel the pressure and excitement building page after page, with nonstop action that keeps you enthralled until the explosive conclusion! Yes. Mack B and his combat teams are living large…and they'll fight against all odds to protect our way of life!

Now you can have all the new Executioner novels delivered right to your home!

You won't want to miss a single one of these exciting new action-adventure And you don't have to! Just fill out and mail the coupon following and we'll e your name in the Executioner home subscription plan. You'll then receive four brand-new action-packed books in the Executioner series every other month, delivered right to your home! You'll get two **Mack Bolan** novels. one **Able Team** and one **Phoenix Force.** No need to worry about sellouts at the bookstore…you'll receive the latest books by mail as soon as they come the presses. That's four enthralling action novels every other month, featuring three of the exciting series included in The Executioner library. Mail the card today to start your adventure.

FREE! Mack Bolan bumper sticker.

When we receive your card we'll send your four explosive Executioner novels and, absolutely FREE, a Mack Bolan "Live Large" bumper sticker! Th large. colorful bumper sticker will look great on your car. your bulletin board anywhere else you want people to know that you like to "Live Large." And yo under no obligation to buy anything—because your first four books come on 10-day free trial! If you're not thrilled with these four exciting books. just ret them to us and you'll owe nothing. The bumper sticker is yours to keep. FRE

Don't miss a single one of these thrilling novels…mail the card now. w you're thinking about it. And get the Mack Bolan bumper sticker FREE !

BOLAN FIGHTS
AGAINST ALL ODDS
TO DEFEND FREEDOM!

Mail this coupon today!

Gold Eagle Reader Service, a division of Worldwide Library
In U.S.A.: 2504 W. Southern Avenue, Tempe, Arizona 85282
In Canada: 649 Ontario Street, Stratford, Ontario N5A 6W2

FREE! MACK BOLAN BUMPER STICKER
when you join our home subscription plan.

YES, please send me my first four Executioner novels, and include my FREE
Mack Bolan bumper sticker as a gift. These first four books are mine to examine free for
10 days. If I am not entirely satisfied with these books, I will return them within 10 days
and owe nothing. If I decide to keep these novels, I will pay just $1.95 per book (total
$7.80). I will then receive the four new Executioner novels every other month as soon
as they come off the presses, and will be billed the same low price of $7.80 per ship-
ment. I understand that each shipment will contain two Mack Bolan novels, one Able
Team and one Phoenix Force. There are no shipping and handling or any other hidden
charges. I may cancel this arrangement at any time, and the bumper sticker is mine to
keep as a FREE gift, even if I do not buy any additional books.

_____

NAME   (PLEASE PRINT)

_____

ADDRESS   APT. NO.

_____

CITY   STATE/PROV.   ZIP/POSTAL CODE

_____

Signature   (If under 18, parent or guardian must sign.)

This offer limited to one order per household. We reserve the right to exercise discretion in
granting membership. If price changes are necessary, you will be notified. Offer expires
September 30, 1983.   166-BPM-PACA

What readers are saying about Able Team

Able Team's fast-moving excitement makes me feel I'm right there and part of the action. I love it!
—V.B.,* Bowling Green IN

The characters are realistic and the weapons accurate. I'm hooked!
—D.B., Greensboro, NC

Able Team is utterly fantastic. To me these books are priceless.
—M.L., Umatilla, OR

I'm an ex-soldier. I marvel at the realism and authenticity of the series. On behalf of my fellow soldiers, thank you.
—M.M., Festus, MI

The style of writing is unique—it comes face-to-face with reality.
—K.L., Powell, TN

The Able Team books gives me a tingling sensation from the beginning of the stories to the end.
—A.S., West Orange, NJ

* Names available on request